T0408823

An Ames County Novel

Seeds of Suspicion

A County Agent Searches for Common Ground

JERRY APPS

LITTLE CREEK PRESS
MINERAL POINT, WISCONSIN

Little Creek Press
5341 Sunny Ridge Road
Mineral Point, WI 53565

ORDERING INFORMATION
Quantity sales. Special discounts are available on quantity purchases
by corporations, associations, and others. For details, contact
info@littlecreekpress.com

Orders by US trade bookstores and wholesalers.
Please contact Little Creek Press or Ingram for details.

Printed in the United States of America

Cataloging-in-Publication Data
Names: Jerry Apps, author
Title: Seeds of Suspicion: A County Agent Searches for Common Ground
Description: Mineral Point, WI Little Creek Press, 2025
Identifiers: LCCN: 2025936254 | ISBN: 978-1-967311-00-2
Classification: Fiction / Small Town & Rural
Fiction / Political
Fiction / Family Life / General

Book design by Little Creek Press

For my late wife, Ruth, who helped
me with all of my writing projects,
including this one.

Contents

1
Broken Window

Iknew the meeting was doomed when the rock came crashing through the window of the Willow River Community Center. Everyone ran outside in the cold, driving rain to see who threw it. I saw a black pickup that I didn't recognize speeding away.

I probably shouldn't have called the meeting in the first place. Tempers had been flaring for several months. What I had hoped to mend would now become more unraveled than ever. Opposing factions hated each other before the meeting; now they would probably blame each other for the rock. I should have seen it coming. I shouldn't have been so sure of myself, of my ability to work through situations like this with everyone coming out a winner. I organized this meeting with the hope of starting a conversation among these groups. I hoped we could find some common areas of agreement and cool off some of the anger that had been festering and building over the past decade—maybe even longer. I hoped that opposing factions might begin listening to each other. They had been good at shouting. Listening would be new to many of them.

I thought an afternoon in early April was a good time to hold a meeting. The snow had mostly melted. The lakes in Ames County, Wisconsin, were beginning to open up, but spring farm work was still a couple of weeks away. The day I picked for the meeting was especially dreary, with a cold rain falling, melting any remaining snow piles, but making outdoor work difficult. I thought I'd done everything right, even down to picking the day. But I was wrong.

My name is Scott Olson, and I'm the county agricultural agent here in Ames County. I'm employed by the county but also by Badger State University's College of Agriculture in Madison, where you'll find agricultural agents, as well as other specialties such as 4-H and Youth, Family Living, and Community Development representing every Wisconsin county. They work as representatives of the university and bring new agricultural and other research findings to the state's citizens and serve as off-campus, non-formal teachers.

I've worked in Ames County for ten years. I was hired right after I finished my master's degree in agricultural journalism when I was twenty-three years old. I'm not one to complain, but lately, as I try to represent the university and Ames County as an off-campus teacher, my job has become increasingly more difficult.

This meeting was a good example. Over the years, I've been involved in plenty of contentious rural issues. Common ones involved an urban couple retiring and moving to our rural county "looking for peace and quiet," only to be awakened on a Sunday morning by a neighbor's enormous tractor roaring across a nearby field. Or they called my office when a skunk decided to find a home under their deck, and I, somehow, should know what to do about it.

These issues were nothing compared to the problems I'm asked to deal with today. Too often I hear, in these contentious debates, "Which side are you on?" I try to explain that I am on the side of scientific information, clear thinking, and reasonable judgment. After trying to explain my role as a county agricultural agent and educator, they listen, but they often don't hear. I offer what I believe is a reasonable explanation, and then, when I think I've done it well, I hear once again, "But which side are you on?"

I had a bad feeling about the meeting before the rock-throwing incident when the large commercial farmers arrived at the community hall wearing bright red shirts that read, "We Feed the World." Sometimes they are referred to as industrial-size farmers. They all sat together on one side of the meeting room. United. Certain that how they farmed was the right way. For them, it was the future of agriculture—the only way to farm.

The "Small Farmers Are Better" group was equally sure of its beliefs and certain that they were right. They all wore green caps emblazoned with the title of their group in large white letters. This group included a widely divergent collection of small-acreage farmers, some farming only two or three acres and none working more than 160 acres. Most of the members of this group saw themselves as environmentalists concerned about the land and soil erosion. Concerned about climate change. Concerned about groundwater pollution and drawing down the aquifer with high-capacity irrigation pumps. Concerned about the proper care of animals. Concerned about the future of the planet.

I should have realized putting these people together in one room was a mistake. They didn't want to listen; they wanted to yell at each other. Each group was certain it was right and wanted to convince the rest of their "rightness." What was I thinking bringing together the industrial-size farmers and the small-acreage farmers? Hate hung over the entire group like an early morning fog. I'd never seen it so intense in my years of working in Ames County.

I walked back inside the now-empty Willow River Community Center. Clyde Jennings, the center's janitor was standing by the broken window, a pile of shattered glass at his feet. In the midst of the broken glass rested the rock that had caused the destruction.

"Don't touch nothin'," Clyde said, a thin, slightly stooped man in his early sixties. I've called the police, and they should be here any minute." He no more than said it when I heard the sound of a siren in the distance. Soon, Willow River's police chief walked through the door. The chief and I had been friends for several years. His department had five officers.

"So, what have we got here?" asked George Wilkins, a former football linebacker at Badger State, was a huge man, maybe six feet five inches and three hundred pounds. His hair had mostly turned gray. He was fair, friendly, and well respected in Willow River and throughout Ames County.

I explained the meeting I had planned. I told him who had turned out and what I had hoped to accomplish. Chief Wilkins knew about the bad feelings these folks had toward each other. He just shook his head as I gave my brief report.

"Before the meeting was half over, this rock came crashing through the window, showering the folks sitting here with broken glass." I pointed to the rock resting in the pile of broken glass with a piece of paper wrapped around it.

"Anybody hurt?"

"I don't think so. After it happened, everybody rushed to the door to leave. Some people probably thought it was a bomb," I said.

"Never know these days," said Chief Wilkins. Could have been a bomb. Country is tearing itself apart. Everybody mad at everybody else. Didn't think the country's anger would make it to Willow River, but it's here. Here in spades."

Chief Wilkins took his phone from his pocket and began taking pictures of the broken window, the pile of shattered glass, and the rock, about the size of two fists, with a piece of paper wrapped around it and a rubber band holding the paper in place.

Clyde, the janitor, stood nearby with his broom in hand, ready to sweep up the mess. While the police chief and I talked, Clyde found a piece of plywood in the storage room large enough to cover the hole in the window.

"You can pick up the rock now," Chief Wilkins said.

I picked up the rock, removed the rubber band and the paper, and began reading:

COUNTY AGENT GUY
YA DAMN GUVMENT AGENTS QUIT MESSIN IN
OUR STUFF
GO BACK TO THE CITY
YOU AIN'T WANTED HERE
THIS A WARNIN

I showed the message to the chief, who read it and shook his head.

"No signature. No way to trace who sent it," the chief said.

"What about fingerprints?" I asked.

"Nah, that's what they do on the TV shows. Chance of a fingerprint on this crunched-up piece of paper is little to none. Besides, I'd have to send the paper off to the crime lab in Madison, and it'd be weeks before we had any results. About all I can say, Scott, is you'd better be careful. Somebody is out to get you. You'd be surprised how many of these anti-government groups we have these days. It's one thing to question what the government is doing, quite another to toss rocks through windows and threaten people."

I didn't know how to respond as a cold chill rolled up my back. "I am a county agricultural agent, a teacher. I'm trying to help people, and I'm threatened because Badger State University and Ames County pay my salary," I said in exasperation.

"Join the club, Scott," the chief said, putting one of his big hands on my shoulder. "You should see the threats that come into the police station—people just plain hate the police these days. See this." Wilkins unbuttoned his shirt and showed me the bulletproof vest he was wearing. "My wife won't let me out the door in the morning without wearing this. It's come to that."

I slowly drove back to my office, the crumpled paper on the seat beside me. My office is in the Ames County Courthouse here in Willow River, only a mile or so from the community center. It takes a lot to shake me up, but I had trouble keeping my trembling hands on the steering wheel of my Ford pickup as I drove down Willow River's Main Street and turned onto Courthouse Drive. I parked in my assigned spot behind the courthouse, took a deep breath, grabbed the piece of paper with the threat, and walked into the historic building.

"Meeting didn't take long," Gladys, our office secretary, said when I walked into my first-floor office in the courthouse. "You not feeling well? You're white as a sheet." Gladys has meticulously combed gray hair and a smile that spreads across her face when she talks. She has worked in our office for thirty years; she began right after completing a business course at Fox Valley Technical College and never married.

She is smart, takes no guff from anyone, and knows about everything that goes on in this office now and for the past thirty years.

I handed her the crumpled piece of paper, which she quickly read.

"Good God," she said. "Where'd you get this?"

"It was wrapped around a rock that someone threw through the window at the community center."

"Good God," Gladys said again, this time loud enough to catch the attention of my colleague, Sarah Frederick, the family living agent with the same employment status that I had and whose office was next to mine. We worked as a team. Both of us were responsible for the 4-H program for young people, and she was responsible for working on a variety of educational programs with families. I worked mostly with agriculture, horticulture, and related programs.

Sarah started working in Ames County the same year that I did. She wears her blonde hair tied in a ponytail and dresses conservatively. She is single and so devoted to her work that people who know her say she has no social life whatsoever.

"Did I just hear that someone threw a rock through the window at the community center with a note attached?" Sarah asked. Her question came out louder than her usual quiet way of speaking.

I handed Sarah the note, which she quickly scanned.

"Scott, this is serious. You show this to the police?"

"I did."

"And ... ?" Sarah said, drawing out the word.

"Chief Wilkins said I'd best watch my back, that this sort of thing was the sign of the times. Not very comforting."

"So, what are you going to do?"

"I don't know." I sat back in my chair, took off my glasses, and closed my eyes.

Why is this happening? Why me? What next? Will someone try to take a shot at me?

2

Ames County Gazette

"Rock Thrown Through Community Center Window"

A meeting of farmers and others with rural interests abruptly ended when someone threw a rock through a window of the Willow River Community Center last Tuesday afternoon. The meeting, called by Ames County Agricultural Agent Scott Olson, had been arranged to discuss the future of farming in Ames County.

Invited to the meeting were representatives from the large commercial farms in the county, both dairy and vegetable farmers. They call their group "We Feed the World." Also invited were members of the "Small Farmers are Better" group. A large rock crashed through a window, spraying several people with broken glass. Everyone left the meeting after the window was smashed. No one was apparently injured.

Willow River Police Chief George Wilkins said, "We are actively searching for the person who threw the rock. So far no one has been arrested." Wilkins asked that if anyone has information about the event to call his office. He further said that he didn't believe the act was caused by a terrorist. "But you never know," he added.

Oscar Anderson and Fred Russo, retired farmers now in their mid-eighties, enjoyed coffee and conversation at the Black Oak Café in Link Lake, just down the road from Willow River. Fred was tall and slim and wore bib overalls no matter where he went or what he did. Oscar was shorter and stockier than his friend and never wore bib overalls to town, but would pull on the trousers he used to wear to church—he hasn't attended church since his wife died. Oscar had a full head of gray hair, was shorter than Fred, and walked with a cane, a result of a farm accident that had him laid up for nearly six months.

Oscar brought the current edition of the *Ames County Gazette* with him.

"You see the *Gazette* this week?" Oscar said, shoving the paper in front of his old friend and neighbor.

"Yeah, I did," said Fred, taking a long sip of coffee and then putting the paper down. "What about it? Lots of cute little kids? Paper does a nice job taking pictures of little kids, especially around Easter."

"Fred, didn't you read the story about the rock smashing through the window over at Willow River?"

"Glanced at it. Didn't read it too careful. Sounded like somebody busted a window at the community center. That kind of stuff happens."

"Geez, Fred. You spend your time looking at pictures in the paper and miss the important stuff."

"So, what's so important about a rock busting a window? It happens."

"You didn't read the story at all. Did you, Fred? Fess up now."

"I said I glanced at it. Didn't sound all that important. Read the headline. Some kind of meeting fell apart. Lots of meetings these days. I hate meetings."

"Fred, this wasn't just another meeting. Our county agent, Scott Olson, was trying to get the big farmers and the small farmers talking to each other."

"I heard those folks kind of hate each other. Did hear that. Big farmers think the little farmers are kind of make-believe farmers, and the little farmers think the big farmers are ruining the environment."

"You heard right, Fred. That's what the meeting was about. And whoever tossed the rock stopped the meeting."

"So, who tossed it?" asked Fred.

"Nobody knows. Police chief in Willow River is working on it."

"Probably a terrorist did it," Fred said, smiling. "Lots of them terrorists around these days. Killing people and doing all kinds of mischief. Bad bunch, them terrorists," Fred said as he took another sip of coffee. "Just never know what a terrorist will do. Just never know. That's what the people on TV say anyway."

"Fred, I don't think a terrorist did it," said Oscar. "Besides, I think you're watching too much TV."

3

Interview

I remember the day I first drove into Ames County. I applied for the assistant county agent job, and I was headed for Willow River, the county seat. I remember driving up Highway 22 and seeing the Ames County sign, and a half-mile or so later, another sign with a big, green four-leaf clover with an H on each leaf and the words, "Ames County 4-H Welcomes You."

It was April, and I would receive my master of science in agricultural journalism from Badger State University in May. I remember the day as cloudy and rather dreary, the trees not yet leafed out, and a few patches of tired, dirty snow remained on the north side of pine plantations I drove past. I saw several large fields, green with what must have been a cover crop and likely a field that would be planted to potatoes later in the month.

I spotted a sign that read "Overlook Park." The park's parking lot, completely deserted on this clear but chilly April day, provided a clear view of the little city of Willow River in the valley below and just beyond it, what I guessed must be Ames Lake. It was a beautiful, peaceful view, even without the big oak and maple trees leafed out. The grass along the roadside was just beginning to show hints of green.

Back in my car on that late Thursday afternoon, I drove by the sign that read, "Willow River, Population 2005," with a thirty-five mile-per-hour speed limit sign next to it. I slowed down, not wanting to get a speeding ticket on my first visit to the town. My job interview wasn't until seven that evening, so I thought I'd look around a bit. See what Willow River, Wisconsin, looked like. I grew up in Green Bay and spent my college years in Madison, both cities many times larger than little Willow River. I guessed it got its name from the little river that snaked through town on its way to Lake Winnebago.

I drove down Main Street, noting a bank, a couple of taverns, a hardware store, a jewelry store, Willow River Public Library, an A&W root beer stand, a grocery store, and a restaurant with the words "Country Cooking Restaurant" on a sign over its door. On the outskirts of town, I drove by the relatively new-looking Willow River Community Center and, a half-mile later, saw the sparkling waters of Ames Lake, with summer homes nearly rubbing against each other along its banks.

I turned my old Ford Fairmont around and headed back down Main Street, where I parked in front of the Country Cooking Restaurant. A little bell tingled when I opened the door and smelled fresh coffee.

"Sit wherever you want," the waitress said. Her hair was mostly gray, and she walked with a little limp. She had a friendly smile. After I was seated, she came over with a pot of coffee, a glass of water, and a menu that she placed in front of me.

"My name is Mable," she said. "Take your time with the menu. Special today is meatloaf for $5.95. It comes with mashed potatoes and green beans. You want some coffee?"

"Sure," I said. "Black coffee, no cream, no sugar."

She tipped the coffee cup in front of me upright and filled it. It smelled good.

Without looking at the menu, I said I would have the special. She took back the menu and said, "Ain't seen you in here before. You new to Willow River?"

"My first time here." I smiled. "I'm here for a job interview."

"Well good luck. Jobs can be a little scarce in these parts. Mostly farmers around here, and a few folks that drive to Wisconsin Rapids where they work in the paper mills, or off to Oshkosh where they have a job in one of the factories there."

She wandered back toward the kitchen and soon returned with my meal—as tasty as I thought it would be. By then, a half dozen or more people had entered the restaurant. Each gave me a quick stare and then looked away. I was clearly the stranger in town, and curious people wondered who I was and why I was there. I ate my meal, not allowing the stares to bother me. I left a dollar tip on the table and walked to the counter where Mable stood by the cash register. I paid and thanked her for a good meal.

"Good luck with the interview," she said as I turned and walked toward the door. The little bell tinkled once more as I exited and returned to my car. I remembered the directions I'd gotten for the courthouse.

"Just drive down Main Street until you come to Courthouse Drive. There's a stoplight at the street intersection—only stoplight in Ames County. Drive down Courthouse Drive, and in a couple blocks you'll see the courthouse on your left. Can't miss it."

I turned at the stoplight, and there was a big old three-story brick building with a statue of what appeared to be a Civil War soldier on the front lawn. I checked the mirror to see if my hair was combed and my necktie was straight. I never wore a necktie, but a friend told me I should do it for a job interview.

Once out of the car, I walked along a tree-studded sidewalk, the limbs still naked after a long winter. I imagined how pretty this walk must be in summer when the entire walkway to the courthouse was shaded. Glancing to my right, I saw another red brick building, two stories, with bars on the windows. The county jail, I surmised.

Pulling open the big wooden courthouse door, I was immediately engulfed with a slightly musty smell and a stronger smell of floor cleaner. Immediately in front of me was the building's directory: Badger State Extension, Rm. 101; Register of Deeds, Rm. 103; County Clerk, Rm. 105; County Treasurer, Rm. 107; and several more entries.

A few steps away I found Room 101 and entered. I was fifteen minutes early for my interview and considerably more scared than

I thought I would be. I pulled open the door and entered the Badger State University Extension Office.

"Can I help you?" a woman working at a computer said. She looked middle-aged and had the biggest, friendliest smile I'd seen in a long while.

"My name is Scott Olson," I said, trying not to sound as scared as I felt. This would be my first formal job interview. I wasn't sure what questions I would get and whether I would have the answers.

"So glad to meet you, Scott. My name is Gladys, Gladys Filinski. We've been expecting you. How was your trip?"

"Easy drive. No problems at all."

"See any deer? Gotta watch out for deer around here. Lots of deer. This time of the year they are moving around, looking for something to eat."

"Nope. Didn't see one deer."

"Well, have a chair. I'll let Otto know you're here. He's our county agriculture agent, as you probably know."

"I haven't met him, but we've talked on the phone a couple of times," I said.

Gladys got up and walked over to a closed door and knocked quietly. I heard her say, "The fellow interviewing for the assistant county agent job is here."

A tall, heavyset man with a full head of graying hair soon appeared in front of me, extending his hand. "Scott, I'm Otto Janson. So nice to meet you."

His handshake was firm and confident; I liked that in a person.

"Let me show you around the office. We've got a few minutes before the interview."

Otto proceeded to show me what would be my office if I got the job. It included an old wooden desk and chair, a mostly empty bookcase, and a couple of wooden visitor chairs, as Otto described them. The only thing on the wall was a calendar, "Compliments of the Willow River State Bank" written in large print across its bottom. The calendar was turned to April, which featured a picture of a farmer plowing a field with a one-bottom plow pulled by a team of horses.

The single window in the room looked out on the courthouse lawn and the statue of the Civil War soldier.

Next, we stopped and looked in an office similar in size to what would be mine but filled with papers piled on all corners of the desk, plus a bookshelf running over with books and several photos of flowers on the wall.

"This is Donna Curry's office; she's our family living agent, at least for another couple months. She plans to retire on July 1. We'll miss her. She's got a lot of friends in Ames County. She's done a great job with the families, both in the country as well as those who live in town."

Otto then showed me the little conference room where we'd be meeting for the interview. It had no windows and mostly featured a long wooden table with ten wooden chairs surrounding it. The walls were covered from floor to ceiling with bookshelves and bulletin racks, where Badger State University's College of Agriculture and United States Department of Agriculture bulletins on every possible subject were prominently displayed. In one corner of the room was a copy machine. And on the wall nearest the door was a metal cabinet.

"Office supplies are in there," Otto said.

"Want to show you something else, a piece of office history." On a lower shelf in the storage cabinet, Otto pulled out a Babcock milk tester and put it on the table.

"Back in the 1920s, the county agent in this office tested milk for farmers—to determine the milk's butterfat content. As you probably know, the butterfat content of a farmer's milk determined the price that the farmer received back in those days. We, of course, don't do that anymore. Milk testing is done in shiny laboratories."

I said I did know that and, in fact, had taken a course at the university where we learned about Steven Moulton Babcock and his famous milk tester and what the invention meant to Wisconsin's fledgling dairy industry at the time. We returned to the outer office, where Gladys was talking with three gentlemen.

Otto immediately introduced me to them.

"Gentlemen, this is Scott Olson, who has applied for the assistant county agent position. We'll be talking with him in the conference room in a few minutes.

"Scott, these men are on the Ames County's Agricultural and Natural Resource Committee, and they will be interviewing you."

"Bill Workman," a big, middle-aged man with calloused hands and a full head of graying hair said as he shook my hand and looked me in the eye. He had brown eyes and a friendly face. "Good to meet you," he said. "Looking forward to chatting with you."

"Hi, Scott, my name is Andy Baird." He shook my hand. He was about my height, a little less than six feet, and was in his early thirties."

"John Flyer," a middle-aged man with a ready smile shook my hand. "Glad you could come today."

Otto, the three committee men, and I walked back to the conference room.

After we all were seated, the questions began. I tried to hide my nervousness but didn't know how well I was doing it. Each of the men had my resume in front of them, which they glanced at on occasion.

"I see you grew up on a farm in Brown County and were born in Green Bay. You a Green Bay Packers fan?"

I said I was, but I hoped if I'd said I preferred the Chicago Bears that wouldn't have disqualified me from the job.

"What kind of farm was it?" asked Bill Workman.

"Dairy farm. We milked about fifty cows when I was growing up. My dad and my brother still farm there."

The questions continued for most of an hour. Questions about my interests, what I thought I could contribute to the Extension program, what I thought about the direction that agriculture seemed to be going and the challenges I saw agriculture facing in the future.

They asked me if I had any questions for them, and I asked how each of them was related to farming and agriculture. "I run a dairy farm. We milk about eighty cows or so, with some hope of expanding when my son and his new wife join in the operation," said Bill Workman.

"Mostly a vegetable farmer," said Andy Baird. "I grow about two hundred acres of potatoes. Have fifty acres of cucumbers, about seventy-five acres of sweet corn."

"I run the John Deere implement business here in Willow River," said John Flyer.

"You a John Deere guy?" he asked, smiling.

"Yup. Pa always had John Deere tractors." I hoped John was joking with his question.

"Well, that's good," said John. Everyone around the table chuckled.

All was going well, and I thought I had answered the questions okay. I was trying to read the faces of the three men and glanced over at Otto, who sat off to the side, not asking questions but listening carefully to what I was saying.

I was expecting, at some point, they would ask about salary, what I was expecting, but they didn't. It was John Flyer who said it. And I was a bit surprised that he did. He began with, "I notice that you will receive a master's degree in May."

"Yes, that's true."

"I feel I must tell you that just because you will have a master's degree doesn't mean we can pay you more."

I was a bit stunned by his answer. I had just spent six years in college, and now I was hearing that the extra two years of education wouldn't mean anything when it came to salary. I tried not to look disappointed, but I didn't respond to what he said. A nervous silence settled over the group. Bill Workman, chair of the committee, finally said, "Scott, would you wait in the outer office so we could talk a bit? It shouldn't be too long."

4
Bill and Paul Workman

I sat in my office thinking about when I was hired and reminiscing about all that had happened from then until now when a knock on the office door brought me back to the present.

Gladys opened the door. She had a concerned look on her face. Over the ten years that Gladys and I have worked together, I have learned to read her facial expressions as various events took place. It wasn't often that I saw this concerned look.

"Bill Workman and his son, Paul, are here to see you," Gladys said.

"Show them in," I said as I quickly piled up some papers on my desk to make it a little neater than it usually was.

"Hi, Bill, Paul. What can I do for you?" I motioned for the father and son to have chairs. I had a pretty good idea why they were here, as they had been sitting in the front row at the community center when the rock came crashing through the window.

Bill Workman began. "Scott, we've known each other for, what is it now, ten years."

"Yup, that's right," I said. "You were chair of the committee that hired me. I remember that day like it was yesterday."

"Well, to put it bluntly. Who in the hell tossed a rock through the window at the community center an hour ago and scared the hell out of everybody in the room?"

"Frankly, I don't know," I answered, wondering where this discussion was headed.

"I'll bet it was one of those tree-hugging, land-loving organic farmers. That's who I think did it," said Paul Workman. Paul was about my age, a big fellow who didn't look at all like his dad. He was bald and could stand to lose forty pounds. He had a reputation for having a short temper and wanted nothing to do with anyone who saw the world differently than he did. I also had a feeling that he really didn't like me.

Recently somebody told me that Paul Workman said he couldn't see why Ames County needed an agricultural agent anymore. He said, "I get my dairy nutrition information directly from the dairy co-op that buys our milk. If I need help selecting seed varieties for our crops, I contact the researchers at the feed and seed companies we work with."

I had heard about Paul's feelings about eliminating my job.

"I want to show you guys something," I said, getting up from my chair, "Excuse me for a minute." I walked to the outer office and retrieved the crumpled piece of paper with the hate message and handed it to Bill, who read it aloud:

COUNTY AGENT GUY
YA DAMN GUVMENT AGENTS QUIT MESSIN IN OUR STUFF
GO BACK TO THE CITY
YOU AIN'T WANTED HERE
THIS A WARNIN

"Where did this come from?" Bill asked as he handed the paper back to me.

"It was wrapped around the rock that sailed through the window at the community center," I said.

"Wrapped around the rock, huh?" Paul said. He was folding and unfolding his hands.

"You show this to the police?" Bill asked.

"I did. They said there was nothing much they could do about it, and I should watch my back."

"Bet it was one of them tree-huggin' organic farmers that did it. Never could trust those guys. Everybody farmed like they do, and we'd all starve to death," offered Paul with a sneer.

"Oh, I don't think an organic farmer did it. I know several of them, and I don't think they would do such a thing," I said. "It's not like one of them to throw a rock through a window."

"So then you think it's one of us 'real farmers'?" Paul said. The expression on his face said it all. So different from his father, who I considered a friend, Paul was a know-it-all, and from the comments I heard about him, he had no use for most government agencies and government programs, including the Badger State University Extension Service. It did cross my mind that Paul and the local Eagle Party, which he and another bunch of folks belong to, could be behind the rock throwing. They were a free market bunch of thinkers who believed that every government program was a waste of "hardworking taxpayers" money. I concluded from reading some of the Eagle Party tirades in the newspaper that unless you agreed with their way of looking at the world, you were the enemy to be ignored at best and eliminated if possible.

"No, I don't think your group did this," I said as I looked at Paul. I don't know who did it, but I'm wondering which way to turn. What I should do next."

Throughout this exchange between Paul and me, Paul's father sat quietly, his cap in his hands. Bill Workman was a clear thinking, open-minded person who took time to make his mind up about something before acting. Sometimes I wondered how he could have raised a son like Paul. Bill was active in the local Farm Bureau and had been its president for several years. He was a good farmer and tried to be a good steward of the land as well. I'm sure he and Paul had many heated discussions about their dairy operation, but that was not my business.

"Scott, I think you are on the right track in trying to bring together the farming folks in Ames County, no matter if they're running a dairy with five thousand cows or growing vegetables for the farmers' market on five acres," said Bill.

"Thank you for saying that."

"We're all in the food production business, and we've got to better understand what each other is doing, how we're doing it, and why what each of us is doing is making an important contribution to society," said Bill.

I looked toward Paul, who was sitting red-faced, wanting to say something but hesitating because he still had some respect for his father and didn't want to contradict him in front of me. That's what I assumed, anyway.

"I'm wondering what I should do," I said. Somewhat afraid of what might happen if I called another meeting, and yet, not wanting to look like one threat would prevent me from doing what I knew needed doing.

"Well, I don't know what to say," offered Bill, who had a worried look on his face.

"I'd suggest you quit trying to bring these groups together," said Paul. "They hate us, and we don't much care for them."

"Now, Paul," his father said, touching him on the arm. "It doesn't hurt to get to know these folks a little better. After all, they are our neighbors."

"Whole project sounds like a waste of time to me," Paul raised his voice as he said it. "They're not gonna change their minds, and we 'real' farmers sure as hell aren't gonna change our minds. What would this world come to if all we had was a bunch of tree-huggin' organic farmers? Tell me, what would the world come to? I'll tell you what would happen. Half the world's people would starve to death. That's what would happen."

Paul stood up, pushed his chair back until it banged the wall, and walked to the door. "I'll be waiting in the pickup," he said as he opened the door and closed it with a bang.

"Scott, I'm sorry about that. Paul's mostly a good boy, and he works hard. But he's got his opinions, and he's also got a temper, as you just saw."

"You don't have to apologize, Bill. These are tough times. I've never seen folks in this country, in this state, in this county, so divided. We used to know how to get along with each other. What's happened, Bill? I don't understand. I just don't. And I wish I knew how to make things better," I said.

"Even though Paul doesn't think so, I appreciate what you're trying to do. I really do. Let me know how I can help. And take care of yourself. There are some crazies out there," Bill said as he stood up and shook my hand. "I better get out to the pickup before Paul drives off without me."

Bill quietly closed the door when he left. I heard him say goodbye to Gladys, who no doubt heard some of Paul Workman's tirade a few minutes earlier.

5
Meeting Discussion

There was a gentle knock on the door, and Gladys walked in. "You okay, Scott?" she asked. "I haven't heard anybody shout at you in a long time. What's going on?"

"Well, apparently Paul hates the small vegetable growers, especially the organic farmers, even more than I thought he did."

"Boy, Paul Workman stormed out of here like he had a bee under his saddle, Gladys said.

"Yeah, you can't believe how different he is from his father. I'm sure glad Paul isn't on the county board. I think his number one goal would be to close down this office," I said.

"You think so?"

"I know so. Paul belongs to the Eagle Party, the bunch that wants to see most of the government disappear. The smaller the government, the better. And according to Paul Workman, we are definitely a part of the government."

"I guess so," said Gladys, shaking her head. "I've been in this office for more than thirty years, and I've never heard talk like this. Shut us down because we're a part of the government? Don't people know all that we do to make things better?"

"Apparently not," I said. "Apparently not."

"Scott, what in heaven's name is going on?" Sarah said as she stood in front of my desk. Sarah was a few years younger than me and had graduated from University of Wisconsin–Stout. She was tall and blonde, with blue eyes that twinkled when she talked. She had a smile so bright you could read by it. Over the years she has had marriage proposals from about every young bachelor in the county. She turned them all down.

"So what are you gonna do, Scott? I saw Bill Workman and his firebrand son were here. That didn't go too well."

"Sarah, there are apparently a lot of people in Ames County who think like Paul Workman. If it was his decision, he would have us closed down in a minute."

"But if we were closed down, what would happen to the 4-H clubs here in the county and all the farm groups and young beginning farmers we both work with? What would happen to them?"

"Sarah, I don't know. I've been trying my best to bring some of these opposing groups together, to get them talking face-to-face and maybe even listening to each other. With this rock-throwing incident, I'll have to start all over again. Start with something new. Something different. Got any ideas?"

"Not at the moment. You have a meeting tonight?"

"I do not."

"Then come over to my place for a glass of wine and dinner, and we can talk. How about six o'clock?"

"I'll be there."

Sarah walked back to her office. I closed my office door and sunk back into my chair. I thought about the courses I'd taken at Badger State University as an undergraduate and a graduate student. I remember courses in chemistry and bacteriology, in botany and zoology where we dissected dead frogs smelling of formaldehyde. I remember psychology and education courses about how to teach adults how to grow alfalfa successfully on acid soils and offered courses in dairy science and animal science. I'd even done practice teaching in five different high schools, where I was learning how to teach high school agriculture students. I remember my courses in agronomy. I had even been on the livestock judging team. I took courses in rural sociology, understanding communities and how they worked, and courses in agricultural economics, where I learned the importance of keeping good financial records and how agricultural markets worked. Agriculture engineering courses introduced me to farm mechanics, basic carpentry, and welding. I took courses in plant pathology, where I learned about plant diseases, and courses in soils, where I learned about fertilization and the prevention of soil erosion. I also had courses in horticulture that encompassed fruit production skills and management problems.

I took all of these courses, and not one came close to preparing me for a hate message wrapped around a rock thrown through a window. Not one course offered me ideas or practical strategies for bringing groups of people who, for various reasons, had developed a distrust of each other and even, in too many instances, a basic, dangerous hatred of each other.

I've got to come up with something to start bringing these groups together. I can't accept being caught in the middle of something. But here I am. Stuck right in the midst of what is shaping up as a rural war. The big guys against the little guys. Add into that an attitude I've read that some city dwellers have toward farmers that ranges from indifference ("as long as our food is cheap") to a belief that every environmental problem, from water and air pollution to soil depletion, is the fault of the farmer. It's a complicated mess.

I drove down the long lane to Sarah's little cabin on Ames Lake that she bought when she first arrived in the county, when lake property was more affordable than it is today. The cabin had two bedrooms, a living room with a small dining room, which both looked out over the lake, plus a tidy kitchen and a bathroom. Simple, neat, and very much like Sarah, its owner. The cabin was also quite isolated. Sarah liked it that way. She was not anti-social; she just wanted to be alone when she was home, to not be bothered by a nosy neighbor. She worked with people all day, every day, sometimes several dozen of them. Her little isolated cabin was her retreat.

I knocked on the door.

"Scott, you don't have to knock. You know that, don't you?" She kissed me on the cheek, took my hand, and led me into her living room, where she had a bottle of merlot along with aged Swiss, five-year-old cheddar, and some crackers—my favorites.

"You look like you need a big glass of wine, maybe more than one," she said, smiling.

"I need more than that."

"After dinner, Scott. After dinner." She took both of my hands in hers and looked right at me. "We'll get through this," she said. "I'll help you. We've been through tough times together, and we'll get through this." Sarah was always the optimistic one in our office, even during tough times, like when Otto Janson retired and they promoted me to agriculture agent and then eliminated my old position so the office would have only two agents rather than three.

"Yup, how could I forget? It was like being promoted and demoted on the same day," I said. "Each of our workloads increased by half, but we made it work."

"That we did, Scott. We're a pretty good team, especially when you consider we've got Gladys in the office. Did you know that she writes down all the unusual calls, letters, and emails she gets and then stuffs them in the bottom drawer of her desk? I picked up a handful of them this afternoon when I left work. Thought they might be fun to read."

Sarah opened her briefcase and took out a handful of note-sized papers.

"Here goes," she said as she unfolded the first note.

"I found this turkey ham in my mother's freezer. It's been there for five years. Is it okay to eat?"

"I make apple cider in the garbage disposal. Is this okay?"

"I use my dishwasher to cook fish. How does that sound to you?"

"Prunes aren't what they used to be. Why is this?"

"I cooked some meat and put it in the refrigerator. Three days later I took it out, and it was green on the bottom. Is it safe to eat?"

By this time I was chuckling as I remembered when Gladys took these questions on the phone, smiling broadly as she listened but sounding very professional when she responded.

"You got to answer most of these questions?" I said.

"Yes, I did, except the one about prunes. Do you think prunes aren't what they used to be?"

"I haven't a clue," I said.

"Here's a call that I remember ending up on your desk," Sarah said, continuing to unfold handwritten notes.

"I bought a house with trees in the yard painted white. The previous owner liked birch trees, so he painted all the trees to look like birch. How do I remove white paint without harming the trees?"

"What'd you tell this person?"

"Frankly, I don't remember. I probably said do nothing, and over time the white paint would fade and disappear. That reminds me of another story. It was during my second year in the county, when I was an assistant county agricultural agent and just learning the ropes. Gladys took this call, and Otto was on another line, and she referred the call to me. It was a woman who said she had a sick crabapple tree, and she wanted someone from our office to come out and 'make my little tree better again.' I drove over to her place; it was on the north side of Willow River, nice little housing area. Still is today. She was standing on her porch waiting for me. First thing she said was, 'You're kind of young, aren't you? You know anything about crabapple trees?' I said I did, not at all sure what I would see when I saw her sick little tree. Well, I was surprised to see the little tree. It was about ten feet tall and had dropped all of its leaves, and it was only July.

"'You can save my little tree? My little Crabby?' the lady asked. She was probably in her sixties, had white hair, and was wringing her hands. 'What spray can you recommend for little Crabby?' She was now gently holding the trunk of Crabby with the most forlorn look on her face. I tried to remember the diseases that commonly affected crabapple trees but quickly decided that no spray would help little Crabby. I told the woman that I would recommend pruning.

"'What kind of pruning?' I said I would recommend pruning little Crabby level with the ground. 'Do you mean destroy my little friend? Do you mean kill Crabby?'

"I told her that her crabapple tree was already dead and should be replaced. Well, I've never forgotten the look on her face. If she'd had a shovel or rake handy, I think she would have hit me with it. I hurried back to the car and then to the office. When I got there, Otto said I should come into his office.

"'Just got a call from a woman who said you were the most incompetent person she'd ever met, and if at all possible, you should be fired. She said you recommended pruning her favorite crabapple tree level with the ground.' Otto said all of this with a straight face. Then he burst out laughing, not allowing me to suffer anymore. He said that what I told her was likely correct, but I needed to work on my garden-side manner a little bit. He laughed even louder.

"We do have the stories, don't we?" Sarah said, chuckling. "Dinner must be ready."

The table was already set in her little dining room that looked through the trees to the waters of Ames Lake. After a dinner of pizza that Sarah had made from scratch and two more glasses of wine, I got up to move back to the living room.

Sarah took my hand and led me toward the bedroom.

6
Scott and Sarah

I pulled into the courthouse parking lot at seven-thirty the following morning. Sarah would come in at eight o'clock. Sarah and I started dating about six months after she arrived in Ames County. It was not a secret, but a good number of people wondered why we had not gotten married. They didn't ask Sarah or me, but they regularly mentioned it to Gladys, who passed the information on to us.

For all practical purposes, Sarah and I are married. In fact, we've been together nearly ten years, which is longer than lots of folks are legally married, and we get along together just fine—at work and not at work. Someday we may get married, but we are too busy with our jobs to think about it now.

I remember the first time we slept together. Sarah had been on the job for six months or so. She was quickly accepted and loved by the farm women with whom she worked, as well as the 4-H leaders in the county. I was up to my ears with my responsibilities, plus helping with 4-H work. I thought, incorrectly, that it was more important to do the work than to waste time reporting what I had done. In those days we were required to file monthly reports of our activities with the district director, Ben Ruskie, my supervisor, who represented

Badger State University. I was three months behind on my reports.

Gladys took the phone call from District Director Ruskie and then put me on the line.

"Scott, you are behind three months with your monthly reports," Ben Ruskie said.

"I know that and I'm sorry."

"Sorry doesn't cut it, Scott. Those reports are due on my desk the end of every month. No excuses. You hear me?"

"But—but I thought the work came first, and the reports could wait."

"Well, the reports can't wait. How do you expect us to get any tax money without well-written reports? Tell me that."

By this time, I didn't know if I should argue with this guy, my boss, who had not spent a day working in a county and didn't know the pressures on county Extension people.

"I'll try to do better," I said, biting my tongue as I said it.

"Well, I hope so." The line went dead.

Sarah happened to be in my office when I took the call. It was late in the afternoon, and we'd just finished a discussion about what we should talk about at the next countywide 4-H leaders meeting, which was held every month from September through May.

"What was that all about?" Sarah asked.

"I just got chewed out royally for being late with my monthly reports."

"Oh," Sarah said. She had likely gotten the same spiel about the importance of filing monthly reports from Ben Ruskie when she was hired. "You don't look so good."

"Don't like being chewed out, especially when I'm working night and day trying to do my best."

"Say, why don't you stop at my place for dinner tonight? I'll open a bottle of wine—and I do know how to cook. You have a meeting tonight?"

"I do not," I said, glancing at my calendar to make sure.

"Then I'll see you around six," Sarah said.

I was feeling sorry for myself. I wasn't accustomed to being reprimanded for what I believed was a rather frivolous reason. Had I screwed up with one of my programs, it would have been appropriate. But being late with a stupid report that I guessed few people bothered to read? What's the world coming to?

I remember the wonderful meal Sarah prepared, the bottle of wine we shared, and her lighthearted way of carrying on a conversation. I remember as I sat across from her how beautiful she was. Her blue eyes sparkled when she talked, and her blonde hair fell easily off her shoulders. I was seeing a side of Sarah Frederick that I had not seen so far. One thing led to another, and I ended up spending the night with Sarah and feeling a bit guilty about it in the morning. I tried to apologize for my actions. She put her finger to my mouth. "No apologies. It was a wonderful evening."

I parked in my assigned parking place in the courthouse parking lot and walked to my office. Gladys was already at her desk.

"Good morning, Scott," she said. "You are looking better than you did yesterday."

"I'm feeling better, Gladys. Feeling a lot better. When Sarah gets in, I'd like for the three of us to chat for a bit about where we can go next with my idea of helping our rural groups get along a little better."

"You sure you wanna do this, Scott, after the warning letter? Sounded like a warning to me. Sounded like this person is out to disrupt or do worse with anything you try next."

"Gladys, I can't let one threatening letter keep me from doing what needs doing. We can't have people who should be on the same page yelling at each other and calling each other names. It's not right. What do our city friends think when they see the farming community so torn apart?"

"I suspect some of them don't care as long as their food is safe, readily available, and cheap," said Gladys.

"That could be. But I have a feeling that a growing number of city folk are concerned about where their food comes from, how animals are cared for, and what's happening to our water."

Just then Sarah walked into the office. "A good morning to the both of you and what a beautiful day it is."

Gladys and I both looked at Sarah, who was smiling broadly.

"Good morning, Sarah," I said, hoping my face didn't show that I had said good morning to a sleepy Sarah a couple hours earlier.

"Could both of you meet in my office in half an hour? I want to share some ideas for where we go next with what didn't work out so well yesterday."

7

Idea Session

With only three of us in the office, I often involved Gladys in our "idea sessions," as both Sarah and Gladys referred to them.

"I got to thinking last night," I said. I glanced at Sarah, who had a strange "what is he going to say next" look on her face. She surely wouldn't want me to say anything about our evening together.

"I talked with the county sheriff a bit after work yesterday. He'd been thinking about the rock throwing, and he told me someone had busted the barn windows on one of the small farmer's properties the previous night. He said I should try again to bring these warring farm groups together."

"Really?" Gladys asked.

"I don't know if this will work, but I'm thinking of organizing a small group. I'm calling it a 'Future of Ag Committee' to work on this problem. With clear heads, I hope a committee can come up with some ideas on how to bring the factions together."

"So, who would you have on this Future of Ag Committee?" Sarah asked.

"Well, I was thinking of asking representatives from the various ag groups, people that I know and who tend to think before shooting off their mouths."

Neither Sarah nor Gladys said anything for what seemed like

forever. Finally Sarah said, "It might work. Just might. At least the ideas they come up with will belong to them and not our office. You won't be blamed if they don't work out. We've got farm people who basically don't trust each other and, in many cases, even hate each other. We've got farm people who don't care much about the government interfering with their lives, passing rules and regulations they've got to follow. We've got folks living here in Willow River who don't care one way or another about farmers. A few think all farmers, big and little, are out to ruin the land and pollute our water."

"All true, Sarah, but we've got to try something. The sheriff is right. Somebody has to do something about the problems we've got here in Ames County. We can't just sit here and let all of this animosity fester. We've got to get people talking to each other. And if we can get a small group doing it, well maybe that will help," I said.

Meanwhile, Gladys, who had more Ames County history in her head than almost anyone else in the county, had said nothing.

"Well, Gladys, what do you think? This an idea that might work?" I asked.

"Wouldn't hurt to try," Gladys said.

"Here are some of the people I suggest. Some were at the first meeting; some were not. I'd start with Bill Workman. He's president of the Ames County Farm Bureau."

"Well," said Gladys, "if you ask Bill Workman, you've got to ask Emil Barnes. He heads up the Farmers Union."

"Agreed," I said. "I've only met Jesse Johnson a couple of times, but we'd better invite him. He's president of the Ames County Vegetable Growers and irrigates about a thousand acres of sweet corn, green beans, and cucumbers just outside of Willow River."

Gladys began jotting down the names.

"I suggest asking Jodi Henderson," offered Sarah. "She's president of the Small-Acreage Farmers Association. As you know, Scott, she and her husband grow around five acres of vegetables just to the west of Willow River. I also heard that she'd spent a couple of years in the military. Some folks think she's a little strange, but I've been impressed with her from the several times we've talked. She's been at several of my meetings where we've talked about developing a farm-to-school program so the schools will have fresh vegetables as part of their school lunch programs. She has a student attending Willow River High School. And you know what? Her son, his name is Josh, is dating Jesse Johnson's daughter, Aimee."

"Is that right?" I said. "At least we've got one example of big and little farmers getting together."

"Yes, isn't young love grand?" Sarah said, smiling broadly.

"Jodi sounds like a good one to add," I said. "But I doubt she'd agree to be part of the group. I think she believes the big commercial farmers are out to get her."

"Well, let's ask her anyway," Sarah said. "I'm sure she and her son have had some interesting talks. Who should we ask from the community who are not farmers?

I think it's important to have these folks represented, as you said earlier."

"A couple of people I'd suggest: John Flyer owns the John Deere dealership, is on the county board, and has been a great supporter of our programs over the years. John is a darn good businessman, too, and levelheaded besides."

"Agreed," said Sarah. Gladys was shaking her head in agreement.

"I hesitate to suggest this next person, but I think we should ask Jeff Miles from the Willow River Bank, your old boyfriend, Sarah." I smiled when I mentioned *boyfriend*, because Sarah had let me know that the flame had long ago gone out between her and Jeff Miles, whom she had dated a few times when they were in college. Jeff began as a farm loan officer a month ago. She scowled at me when I mentioned his name. Gladys smiled, knowing that Sarah did not want to be reminded of what she had been doing in college. Gladys told me Jeff had called the office several times the first week he was here, wanting to talk with Sarah. Gladys had said she didn't know whether Jeff and Sarah had talked.

"It makes sense to add the bank's loan officer to the mix. Don't you agree?" I said, looking at Sarah with a straight face.

"Okay," was all Sarah said. She was not smiling, but Gladys was.

Sara continued, "How about adding Harvey Rivers? He's president of the Ames County Historical Society and its Farm Museum. Harvey's group knows the history of farming in this area and could offer some good background."

"Sure," I said. "Write down his name."

"And, of course, we should add Greg Charter, editor of the *Ames County Gazette* to the group. He's always done a good job reporting on our various events." I looked at both of my colleagues, and they were shaking their heads in agreement.

"Okay. Any pitfalls in putting together a group like this?" I asked.

"Probably lots of them, but we won't know until we try. Some of these folks might even turn us down. Wouldn't surprise me if they did," Sarah said. "Don't you think we should ask Jill Varsac? She lives here in Willow River and is the regional president for Citizens for the Future, the environmental group. She came to one of my meetings once—her group can be a little obnoxious and self-righteous at times, and we all know that CFTF mostly hates agriculture, especially large-scale farming."

"Geez, I don't know, Sarah. Do you think she would agree to be with this group? Besides, as I think about it, I'm wondering if someone from the CFTF threw the rock through the window the other day. They've been known to do stuff like that."

"That could be, but I think we should invite her anyway."

"Okay. Guess it wouldn't hurt to ask her," I said. I had never met Jill Varsac, but I had surely heard about her and her group. She was on the radio and television nearly every week and in the state newspapers at least once a month with a complaint about how agriculture was polluting the air, using too much water, or generally ruining the environment for future generations.

"I think she should be a part of the group," Sarah said once more. "Especially if we want all factions represented."

"Anybody else?" I hesitated for a moment but got no response. "Alright then. I'll get on the phone and see how many of these folks will accept our invitation. By the way, anyone got a better name for this group than the Future of Ag Committee?"

"How about calling this an Agricultural Planning Council?" offered Sarah. "Sounds a lot more important and impressive than 'committee.'"

"Okay by me," I said. "Who can turn down an offer to be part of a planning council?"

"We'll soon find out," said Gladys.

I immediately began calling the names on the list, beginning with those I knew well, such as Bill Workman, Emil Barnes, and Greg Charter from the newspaper. I knew that if these men agreed to be on our new planning council, the rest of the people on the list would also agree to serve. The cynical side of me reasoned they wouldn't want to be left out of the decisions these other folks were making. And I was right. Everyone agreed to serve. I told them that the council's purpose was to plan the future direction of Ames County's agriculture and that Gladys would be in touch with them soon to set up a date when we could meet. I hoped it would be within the next two weeks.

8

Agricultural Planning Council

"Thank you so much for coming," I said at the first meeting of the Agricultural Planning Council. It had been two weeks since I organized the group. "I know that those of you who are farmers are busy with spring work. Several of you were at the community center meeting a few weeks ago when someone tossed a rock through the window, closing down the meeting. Thanks for coming to that meeting, and I'm sorry it ended like that."

"Terrible, just terrible. I never saw anything like that happen here in Ames County. Still wondering who did it?" asked Bill Workman.

"I wish I knew. The police are looking into it. I'm hoping they'll find out who the culprit is. But in the meantime, we've got to move on." I continued, "We organized this planning council to see where we might go next in solving some of the problems we face in our community these days. I want your ideas on what we might do. But first we need to spend a few minutes introducing ourselves. I'm sure many of you know each other, but many of you do not. Most of you know Bill Workman. Say a word or two about yourself, Bill."

"Well, I'm a dairy farmer. My son and I milk about eighty cows. I'm also president of the Ames County Farm Bureau."

"Jeff, you're next. I know you are new to Ames County." This was the first time I'd met Jeff Miles. I'd meant to stop at the bank and introduce myself, but with everything going on, I hadn't gotten around to doing it.

"My name is Jeff Miles, and I'm the new agricultural loan officer at the Willow River Bank here in Willow River. I've been here about a month. Previously I worked as loan officer for a bank in Dunn County, but I'm very pleased to be here and have a chance to meet all of you and be a part of this planning council." Jeff was short and a little plump and had a bit of an arrogant look about him as I watched him introduce himself to the others in the room. I thought to myself, *What did Sarah see in this guy?* But that was years ago.

Jeff turned to the middle-aged woman sitting next to him. She had short black hair and big brown eyes.

"I'm Jodi Henderson. I'm president of the Small-Acreage Farmers Association here in Ames County. We have about sixty members, with more joining each year. Our members are mostly vegetable farmers, who grow vegetables for the farmers' markets in the area, as well as for several school lunch programs and a number of restaurants as well."

"I'm president of the Ames County Farmers Union," said Emil Barnes, who was sitting next to Jodi and had been chatting with her before I called the meeting to order. In his sixties, Emil was mostly bald and smiled a lot when he talked. He walked with a bit of a limp.

"Jesse Johnson," said a heavyset, deeply tanned fellow who appeared to be in his forties. "I'm president of the Ames County Vegetable Growers."

"John Flyer is my name. My family owns the John Deere dealership here in Willow River. We've been here since 1931 and hope to be here for many more years." Flyer is a friendly fellow in his mid-forties who meets everyone with a smile and a hearty handshake.

"I'm Jill Varsac. I'm regional president of the Citizens for the Future—CFTF for short." Jill was scarcely five feet tall and "thin as a rail," as Bill Workman later described her. But she had a big voice and spoke with confidence.

"Harvey Rivers," said a tall, thin man in his early sixties. "I'm president of the Ames County Historical Society. Glad to be a part of the group."

"I guess I'm last," said Greg Charter, the editor of the *Ames County Gazette*, who sat at the end of the table and was busy taking notes as the various members of the group introduced themselves. "Before we all leave today, I'd like to take a group photo," Greg said. "I'll also write an article about this group, and as we work along, I'll keep people informed about what we are doing."

"Thanks, Greg," I said. Greg was about my age, maybe a little older. To see him, you'd guess that he had slept in his clothes, and he never bothered to comb his hair. But when you read his words, you were immediately impressed with his knowledge and his uncanny ability to make something complicated easily understood. Besides that, I considered him a good friend.

"Well, that takes care of the introductions. Thanks for taking time to do that," I said. "I'm hoping we can meet as a group every couple of weeks or so for a few months, with the hope that we'll come up with ideas that may help all of us understand each other's perspective a bit better."

Several heads nodded in agreement. "What I'd like to do today is some brainstorming to see what possible ideas you all might have." I walked up to the whiteboard with a dry-erase marker in hand.

"One obvious event that's coming up is the June Dairy Month Breakfast, which Emil knows all about because it's at his farm." I nodded to Emil when I said it and proceeded to write "June Dairy Month Breakfast" on the whiteboard.

"Can we do something at the breakfast?" I asked. "It usually draws upwards of three hundred people; most are townspeople who look forward to a morning in the country."

"Well, I agree this would be a good time to do something," said Jodi Henderson.

"I have an idea," said Harvey. "How about I set up a little display of old-time farm equipment that I can bring from our museum out to your farm, Emil? I could use a little help in setting up the display."

Several hands went up, indicating they'd help with the historical display.

"Along those lines," offered John Flyer, "I've got several old John Deere tractors that I could bring out to your farm. I've got an old John Deere A. Got a B, too, and I could even bring out our big old diesel R that I haven't started up for a while. People like to see old tractors."

"Sounds like a good idea," said Bill. "I grew up driving a John Deere B on the home farm. I've never forgotten the sound of that two-cylinder engine. Sounds just like an old partridge drumming on a log."

"I'm working with Emil to make posters about his operation. How many cows do you milk these days, Emil?" I asked.

"Somewhere around seventy-five."

"People want to know how much milk a cow can give in a day, how much feed they eat, how much water they drink—those kinds of questions. They also don't know the breeds. Yup. Lots of folks these days don't know a Holstein from a Jersey," I said. "Emil is part of a group that turns his cows out to pasture as soon as the pasture's green up, which is soon. We'll have a poster about pasture grazing as well."

"That all sounds good to me," said Jodi. "I imagine you can use some help at the breakfast itself, maybe helping prepare pancakes. I'm a pretty good pancake maker."

"Thank you," said Emil. "We've got our local 4-H club helping out, but we're always short of volunteers. You will be more than welcome at the pancake grill."

The only member of the group who didn't offer to volunteer to work at the breakfast was Jesse Johnson. He probably had a good reason, but I didn't ask. I knew he would be busy on his big vegetable farm.

With the brief discussion of the dairy breakfast completed, I said, "Okay, I'd like to spend the rest of this first meeting brainstorming a bit about what other kinds of activities we could do to help our various farming groups better understand what each other is doing and help the general public appreciate a bit more where their food comes from. Any ideas?"

"What if we organized a big farm-city picnic? We could call it that and invite farmers and their families, tourists, and city folk with their kids. Make it a big day. Get a polka band to play. Have games for the kids," offered Greg Charter.

I wrote "Farm-City Picnic" on the whiteboard.

"How about a special Farm History Day at our museum? I'm sure our group would be happy to sponsor and help with putting it on."

"Sounds good to me," I said as I wrote "Farm History Day at museum" on the whiteboard.

"Can we sponsor some special events and displays at the county fair, maybe with a theme: 'The source of your food.' Something like that?" offered Jodi.

I wrote down "County fair events and displays."

"My kids are in 4-H," said John Flyer. "What if we sponsored a speaking contest for 4-H members featuring Ames County agriculture?"

I wrote "4-H speaking contest."

"How about some farm tours, to see our dairy farms, to see what our vegetable growers are doing, and to see what the small-acreage people are doing?" suggested Jesse Johnson.

I wrote down "farm tours" and was pleased to hear the suggestion from Jesse, who had said little at the meeting so far.

"What else?" I asked, looking around the room. "Jeff, you've been quiet. You're new here in the county. What have you seen other places doing?"

"Well," said Jeff, rubbing his chin. "Up in Dunn County the local historical society organized a group of retired people to write down their stories of what farming was like when they were kids. Got some really interesting stories."

I wrote "Early farming stories."

"Jill, any ideas that you'd like us to consider?"

"I think we should make sure to include something about farming and the environment in some of the events we've already talked about. Especially at the county fair."

"Good idea," I said. "Anything else?" I paused with my dry-erase marker in hand, but everyone was quiet.

"Okay, that's probably enough for our first meeting—somewhere along the line I suggested we wouldn't meet for more than an hour because I know how busy you all are. And it's been about an hour. Here's what I suggest. Think about these ideas." I went over the list that I had written on the board:

Possible Activities and Events
June Dairy Month Breakfast
Farm-City Picnic
Farm History Day at museum
Special activities at county fair
4-H speaking contest
Farm tours
Early farming stories

"At our next meeting we'll discuss them and see where we might go from here. Any questions?"

"When's the next meeting?" asked Bill.

"How about three weeks from today? Same time, same place."

I watched as people fumbled around for their pocket calendars and smartphones. Unbelievably, everyone said they could make it.

"And before we go, I'd like to turn running the meeting over to a different person each time we meet. Jodi, would you agree to chair the next meeting?"

"Sure," Jodi said. "I'll give it a try."

"Don't forget the group photo," said Greg as he dug his camera out of the bag he always carried.

9
Dairy Breakfast Planning

Driving to work the following morning, I was feeling good. When I left my two-bedroom apartment—the same one I rented when I first moved to Willow River—I stopped to listen to the birds singing. My apartment building was only a few blocks from Willow River Memorial Park, located right on the lake, which was wooded and had lots of early spring bird talk. I also noticed that the maples were beginning to leaf out, and huge patches of wildflowers were beginning to appear where only a few weeks ago, I saw lingering piles of dirty, tired snow.

Sitting at my desk in my office, I was thinking about yesterday's meeting. No one was shouting. No one was trying to blame someone for something. I saw some cooperation in the group that I knew didn't always see things in the same way. I'm sure plenty of issues lay beneath the surface and would surely come to the top as we continued meeting. I expected that and, in some ways, looked forward to it. In my experience, talking face-to-face accomplishes so much more than Tweets, anonymous stories on Facebook, letters to the editor, and a flurry of radio, TV, and newspaper rants.

I knew the dairy breakfast was a good idea, but my mind turned back to the rock-throwing incident a few weeks ago. Could someone try to disrupt the breakfast? I decided to talk to Police Chief Wilkins about this, to get his take.

I dialed his direct number.

"Wilkins here," he answered. He had the gruffest phone voice of anybody I'd ever known.

"It's Scott Olson," I said, wondering if Wilkins was having a bad day and would growl at me.

"Oh, Scott, how are things going? Any more threats?"

"Not so far," I said. "But I wanted to give you a heads up on the dairy breakfast we're planning at the Emil Barnes's farm on Saturday, June 10. You know where that is?"

"I do," said the chief. "He's got a nice place."

"Maybe I'm a little paranoid, but the breakfast would be a good place for somebody to do some mischief—or worse."

"Never can tell what those crazies will do," said the chief. "I'll talk to my officers, and I'll give the sheriff a call, too. Maybe he can send some deputies to make sure everything goes well."

"Thanks, Chief. Thank you very much. I've never forgotten the old saying: Plan for the best, but prepare for the worst."

"It's good advice," the chief said. "Anything else?"

"Well, I must ask, know anything more about who tossed the rock through the window at the community center and sent me the hate letter?"

"Nope. Nothing yet, but we're working on it. I can't remember when anyone around here got a threatening letter."

A couple of mornings later, Gladys stopped at my desk when I arrived at the office.

"Just got the new issue of the *Ames County Gazette*. You made the front page," she said as she dropped the paper on my desk. I picked it up and read:

"New Ames County Agricultural Planning Council Formed"

With the leadership of Scott Olson, Ames County agricultural agent, a new group of agricultural leaders and others with agricultural and rural community interests has been formed.

The group is called the Ames County Agricultural Planning Council. Council members include Bill Workman, president of the Ames County Farm Bureau; Jodi Henderson, president of the Small-Acreage Farmers Association; Jesse Johnson, president of the Ames County Vegetable Growers; Harvey Rivers, president of the Ames County Historical Society; Jeff Miles, agricultural loan officer for the Willow River Bank; John Flyer, Willow River, John Deere dealer; Emil Barnes, president of the Ames County Farmers Union; Jill Varsac, regional director for the environmental group, Citizens for the Future; and Greg Charter, editor of the Ames County Gazette.

The council plans to meet regularly for the next several months to plan activities that will bring together the divergent interests of the small and large commercial farmers, along with environmental groups concerned about today's farming approaches. The group agreed to help out at the June Dairy Month Breakfast, which will be held at the Emil Barnes Farm on Saturday, June 10. The group also suggested that retired farmers, both men and women, submit stories of what farm life was like in Ames County fifty-plus years ago. A selection of these stories will be published in the Gazette.

Above the story was a half-page photo of the group. Some smiling, some not. *It's a start*, I thought. At least we got the group to sit down together without anyone yelling at each other.

Fred and Oscar were enjoying their morning coffee at their usual table at the Black Oak Café after turning down the café's giant sweet rolls.

"Well, what do you think?" asked Oscar.

"About what?" answered Fred. "I think about a lot of stuff. My head is full of thoughts. More than I can handle some days."

"About the article in the *Gazette*: the new ag planning council the county agent has organized?"

"Yeah, I did see that. Probably a good idea. Lots of people mad at each other. Too bad. We all used to get along—well, mostly. Once in a while we got it in for somebody. That happens, you know. But lots of folks are mad about something or other these days."

"Did you read the whole article, Fred?" asked Oscar, taking a big sip of coffee.

"Probably not. Got the gist of it, though. Lots of stuff to read these days. Figure getting the gist of something is better than nothing at all. Wouldn't you say, Oscar?"

"I suppose. But sometimes I think it's important to read something all the way through. Anyway, did you see that this planning council is asking old-timers like us to write down what farming was like years ago?"

"Really? Why'd they suggest that? Thought they were worried about tomorrow, not yesterday."

"Well, they are worried about tomorrow, but what I've always said, you can't know where you're going unless you know where you've been," said Oscar, smiling.

"I have heard you say that, Oscar. So, what's your point?"

"My point is we ought to write down some of what we remember about farming back when we were kids," said Oscar.

"Who'd give a rat's behind about what farming was like when we were kids? That's one helluva long time ago. Geez, I remember when my old man taught me how to drive a horse. Nobody had tractors in those days. I don't think I was much more than ten years old, and I was driving old Daisy on a one-row cultivator, digging up weeds between the potato rows. Yup, I remember that just like it was yesterday. Was damn hard work for a kid. But we did learn how to work, didn't we, Oscar? We all learned how to work."

Fred took a long drink of coffee.

"Fred, that's just the kind of stuff you should write down and send to the *Gazette.*

"Nah, I ain't no writer. I'm a talker. There's a difference between a talker and a writer. But take you, Oscar. You're both a talker and a writer—yes, you are."

"Well, thank you. That's good of you to say. Most folks these days say I'm mostly full of B.S."

"You do have a little of that, too," said Fred, grinning from ear to ear.

"I was thinking about doing a story about what it was like before we got electricity on our farm, which we didn't get until 1947. What it was like farmin' with kerosene lamps and lanterns," said Oscar.

"You think anybody's interested in that? Back then, without electricity, winter nights were plenty dark and long."

"We'll find out. That's what I'm gonna write about. And you should write something, too, Fred. Folks today just don't know what farmin' was like in the good old days, which mostly weren't all that good."

10
Dairy Breakfast

The Saturday of the June Dairy Month Breakfast dawned with a bright sun, not a cloud in the sky. I got up early and drove out to Emil Barnes's farm so I could help set up for the big breakfast, which in past years would draw a couple hundred people and sometimes more, depending on the weather. With a day like this, with a prediction of seventy degrees by noon, I wouldn't be surprised that we'd see three or four hundred people.

I noticed two sheriff's deputies directing traffic. I wondered how many more officers I'd see. Chief Wilkins, true to his word, didn't want any repeat of what happened at the meeting where a rock crashed through the window of the meeting room.

Emil's farm was a showplace. The kind of farm that when you drive by, you say, that's what Wisconsin is all about. He was still using the old red barn built back in 1900 when the dairy industry was just beginning to take over as a major agricultural enterprise in the country. Today, Emil uses the old barn as a shelter for his heifers.

Twenty years ago or so, he built a free-stall barn for his milk cows and a milking parlor where they were milked morning and early evening. Different from the dairy farms that were much larger than his, his cattle grazed on pasture from April until October, depending on the weather. He only kept them confined in the barn during the cold winter months. Of course, they came back from the pasture to the barn for some ground grain that they ate to supplement what they were eating in the pasture and to be milked.

When I arrived at six-thirty, one of Wilkins's deputies greeted me at the sign-up table, where people were asked to pay five dollars for their breakfast. I noticed another officer standing by the collection of antique farm machinery and still another standing near the free-stall barn, where I had erected several signs the previous day. One sign had a photo of a Jersey cow with a brief description of that breed.

Several members of the planning council were there and helping to put the final touches on the setup, which had been mostly done the previous day. Everyone seemed in good spirits.

People of all ages began arriving. By eight o'clock every table in Emil's big machine shed that he had cleared out for the event was filled. People happily feasted on stacks of pancakes that Jodi Henderson was preparing with the help of a cadre of 4-H members. I saw Jeff Miles piling slabs of ham on people's plates. Next to him, Bill Workman and Jill Varsac worked at a huge skillet filled with sizzling scrambled eggs.

I wasn't surprised to see Jesse Johnson's daughter, Aimee, at the breakfast with Jodi Henderson's son, Josh. They obviously were having a good time, chatting with each other. When they finished breakfast, they held hands while looking at the old farm machinery and inspecting the loose-tie cow barn. I was pleased to see these young people decided they could be together even though their parents farmed in very different ways. Jesse was a multi-thousand-acre vegetable grower. His farm depended heavily on deep-well irrigation to grow his crops. While Jodi was a small-acreage vegetable grower who farmed a fraction of the acres that Jesse did.

After finishing their breakfast, I noticed a group of older farmers gathering around the display of antique farm machinery that Harvey Rivers had brought. I saw a walking plow, a spring-tooth drag, a hand-cranked corn sheller, and an old Monitor pump engine that Harvey had cranked up. I had always enjoyed the sound of these old farm engines that many farmers had before electricity came to their farms. I listened to gray-haired farmers explaining to their grandkids how they had once used this equipment.

One of John Flyer's antique John Deere tractors was hooked to a wagon, and he was taking people on a tour of Emil's farm, showing them where the cattle grazed and how the pasture was divided so that the sixty-five grazing cattle had fresh pasture every day. I overheard Emil explain this before the wagon load of families headed off on the tour. I heard the *pop, pop* of the two-cylinder tractor as it labored just a bit with each load of visitors as they climbed the little rise just back of the free-stall barn where the cattle returned each morning and night for their grain ration and to be milked.

Promptly at nine o'clock I took the microphone, and before introducing Emil Barnes and his wife, I said a few words about the new Ames County Agricultural Planning Council. I introduced each council member by asking them to hold up their hands. All were helping out at the breakfast except Jesse Johnson, who had another commitment. I think people were a little surprised that each person I introduced had a job, from making pancakes to frying eggs and dipping ice cream. I noticed that nearly everyone lined up for a bowl of ice cream topped with fresh strawberries after breakfast. I also noticed that two police officers were standing off to the side, their eyes on the crowd that had gathered in front of the farm wagon I was using as a stage.

"Our hosts today are Emil Barnes and his wife, Eleanor," I began. "Let's give them a big round of applause for so graciously allowing us to hold this June Dairy Month Breakfast at their farm. I also want you to know that Emil is one of the members of the Ames County Agricultural Planning Council."

When the applause died down, I handed the microphone to Mrs. Barnes, who had said she wanted to say a few words.

"I'm so pleased to see all of you on this beautiful June morning," she began. "Emil and I are always glad to have visitors, and if any of you want to come back on another day, give me a call, and we'll arrange it. I'll turn the microphone over to Emil. Thanks so much for coming this morning. I'm especially pleased to see so many children." She handed the mike over to her husband.

"Let me join Eleanor in welcoming you to our farm. We are genuinely pleased to see so many of you on this beautiful June morning. Some of you have been asking about our operation, and I'll take a minute to share a few things. First, this farm has been in our family for more than a hundred years. My grandfather started farming this land in 1917. It was my grandfather who built this big red barn right over there." Emil pointed to the barn. "In the early days, he milked cows by hand in that barn. I believe twenty milk cows were the most he ever had. But as you might guess, milking twenty cows by hand, by the light of a kerosene lantern, was no small task. Today we have sixty-five milk cows, all Jerseys, and we belong to the Wisconsin Grazers organization, a group of farmers who continue to allow their cattle to graze on pasture land. As you probably know, compared to some dairy farms that have a thousand cows or more, we are a small operation. These larger dairy farms keep their cattle inside year-round and haul their feed to them. We've chosen to remain smaller and are committed to having our cattle spend a good deal of their time outside, on pasture. If you have any questions, just come up to me and ask. And thanks again for coming."

I stopped briefly at my office later that afternoon after I'd helped the crew clean up at the Barnes farm. I was elated with how everything had turned out. The person selling tickets said five hundred people had attended—an amazing crowd. I was more than pleased with how the members of the planning council all dove right in and helped with the event. People who previously had little to do with each other, like Jill Varsac and Bill Workman, were working together. And Jodi Henderson's son, Josh, with Jesse Johnson's daughter, Aimee, enjoying the breakfast and each other.

We were on our way toward resolving some of the animosity these groups had toward each other. I breathed a sigh of relief that no one tried to disrupt the breakfast. Who knows? Someone may have had that in mind, but the police presence may have deterred them. I was looking forward to a relaxing Sunday. Maybe Sarah and I could sneak off to Oshkosh for dinner and maybe see a movie.

11
Another Hate Letter

On Monday morning I couldn't have felt more upbeat. The dairy breakfast had been a huge success—no disruptions whatsoever. And Sarah and I had a great time in Oshkosh.

I was busy working on the dreaded activity report I had to regularly submit to Ben Ruskie. If a report was as much as a day late, I heard from Ruskie—as did every other Extension agent in the district who committed the most egregious error.

I heard someone in the outer office crying. Looking up from my report writing, I saw Aimee Johnson through my open office door. In between sobs, I heard her ask if Sarah was in. After learning she was, Aimee entered Sarah's office and closed the door. I wondered what was going on. I'd just seen Aimee on Saturday at the dairy breakfast, and she was the picture of happiness as he saw her holding hands with Josh and enjoying the beautiful morning. I remembered that Aimee was an active 4-H member and helped Sarah with several special programs for younger girls in 4-H.

A short time later I heard Aimee leave, and Sarah walked into my office and closed the door.

"I suspect you are wondering what that was all about?" Sarah asked.

"Yes, I guess I am. What's got young Aimee Johnson so torn up?"

"Well, it's kind of a sad story. Aimee told me that she and her boyfriend, Josh, had such a good time at the dairy breakfast. And between sobs, she told me how much she really loved Josh and how he was such a nice guy and how she wanted to spend more time with him."

"Yes," I said, waiting to hear what brought on all the tears and her visit to our office.

"Well, when Aimee got home from the farm breakfast on Saturday, all hell broke loose," said Sarah.

"What happened?"

"Aimee's dad was furious when he heard that his daughter had gone to the dairy breakfast with Josh without asking his permission. Aimee said she had planned to ask her father, but he was never around. That he was always off somewhere in his pickup checking on irrigation wells, making sure that the farm crew was doing what Jesse wanted them to do and a host of other necessary tasks."

"Sounds like he didn't have much time for his daughter," I said. "Did she tell her mother she was going to the breakfast?"

"She did, but her mother was afraid to pass the information along to her dad because, as Aimee said, 'I think Mom's afraid of Dad because he has a terrible temper.'"

"So, what did Aimee want this morning?" I asked, still curious but guessing what must have happened.

"She needed someone to talk to. Her dad told her that she had broken a family rule about asking his permission whenever she went out on a date and that she should never be seen with that Henderson kid again."

"Know what else he told her?" asked Sarah.

"I can only guess."

"He told her that he wanted her to date a real farmer and that small-acreage farmers, like Josh's family, were only playing at farming. He told her, 'If all farmers farmed like the Henderson family, it wouldn't be long before everyone starved.'"

"Wow," I said. "And I thought we were beginning to make some progress in having the different farmer groups come to understand

and accept each other. Sounds like we've got a long way to go."

"Sure does," said Sarah. "And young people like Aimee and Josh are caught right in the middle of it all."

"Well, at least we've got Jesse as a member of the planning council," I said. "He hasn't said much, and he didn't show up at the dairy breakfast to help out, but I hope he stays on. Can't help but feel sorry for Aimee and Josh." I shook my head.

My good feelings about what we accomplished at the dairy breakfast were dashed a bit. We obviously had a long way to go in merely bringing our agricultural community together, to say nothing about having the general public learn a bit more and appreciate what farmers do and the challenges they face.

Sarah returned to her office, and I returned to writing my activity report when a stone-faced Gladys entered my office. The moment I saw her face, I knew something was dreadfully wrong. It wasn't the happy face I saw every day in the office.

"Just opened the mail," she said. "This came." She handed me an envelope addressed to "COUNTY AGENT GUY, COURTHOUSE, WILLOW RIVER, WISCONSIN.

"I read the letter, and I'm scared," Gladys said. "Scared for you."

I walked into my office, sat down at my desk, and unfolded the single sheet of paper with all boldfaced words scrawled across the page:

COUNTY AGENT GUY
YOU DUMB OR SOMETHING
YOU AIN'T WANTED AROUND HERE NO MORE
BUSTED WINDOW NOT GET YOUR ATTENTION
IF YOU AIN'T GONE OUTTA HERE AND SOON
WELL, YOU AIN'T SEEN NOTHIN SO FAR
YOU GETTIN' WORRIED YET?

I walked out to where Gladys sat at her desk.

"This is really something," is all I could think to say. "Really something."

"Want me to call the police chief?" Gladys said.

"I suppose." I returned to my office and read the letter once more.

"What's going on, Gladys?" asked Police Chief Wilkins as he walked into the office fifteen minutes later and greeted Gladys. She showed the chief into my office, where I handed him the new piece of hate mail.

"This came in the mail this morning," I said as I handed the letter to the chief.

"Wow. Wonder who sent this? Sounds like the same guy who sailed a rock through the window at your meeting a few weeks ago," said Wilkins.

"Sure does. Just when I thought we were past this kind of stuff. The dairy breakfast came off without a hitch. I said it before, and I'll repeat it. Thanks so much for having officers at the breakfast."

"You are welcome. But let's get back to this guy. I'm assuming it's a guy. He hasn't come right out and said he'd harm you in any way, but he sure hints at it," the chief said, shaking his head. "Can't believe this kind of thing is going on here in Ames County. People getting threatening letters. You know anybody that you've ticked off recently? Remember anybody like that?"

"I really don't. Suppose I do make one group or the other mad at me when I lay out some agricultural facts that they don't like. I know some of the more vocal members of the small farmers' group aren't too happy that I appear to be supporting the industrial-size farmers. And I know that the industrial-size farmers can't understand why I would waste my time with the small-acreage farmers. Occasionally there is a letter to the editor calling me out for doing that. This environmental group, CFTF, they've been on my case for ten years. Just met Jill Varsac, who heads up that group—she seems sensible enough. Some of their members can be a little extreme sometimes."

"I know the group. Seems they are protesting one thing or another all the time, but I've got my fingers crossed. They haven't done anything close to what might be called violent, at least not here in Ames County," said Wilkins.

"George, I work for the university as well as for Ames County, and it's my job to help everyone—to bring the university to all the people.

I've tried to do that ever since I've been here. I've had lots of people yell at me. Just the other day, Bill Workman's son, Paul—you probably know him—stood right in this office telling me real farmers didn't need this Extension Office anymore. But that's not all that unusual. In this business it happens. You can't please everybody."

"Tell me about it," the chief said. "You want me to talk with Paul Workman, see what he has to say about all this, see if maybe he's behind these letters?"

"No, I don't think so. His father, Bill, is one of my big supporters. Bill would feel awful if he thought his son was doing this stuff. I don't think he's the one. I really don't. But what do I know," I said. "Frankly, I'm worried, George. What should I do?"

"Well," Chief Wilkins said, rubbing his chin. "I've never dealt with anything like this before. I don't know." He stopped again and scratched his head. "So far, there's no real threat of bodily harm to you."

"So far," I repeated.

"I don't know what to say, other than watch yourself. And if you get another letter like this, let me know right away, and we'll see if we can figure this thing out. Could be this is just some guy that's more than a little mad at you, and it's his way of letting off steam. Why don't you make a copy of both the letters you got and give the originals to me. I'll send them to the crime lab in Madison and see if they can tell us anything—give us a clue as to who is doing this. May take a while to hear, but I think I'd better do this."

I asked Gladys to make a copy of this newest letter as well as the previous one and give the originals to Chief Wilkins.

"Keep in touch," the chief said as he left my office.

What started as a perfect day had quickly turned into a continuing nightmare. Maybe I'm a bit paranoid, but when I read the letter, it surely sounded like whoever wrote it had given me an ultimatum: either leave Ames County, or my life would be in danger. That's how I read it, anyway.

Gladys brought me the copy she made of the letter and put it on my desk. I read it again, trying to figure out who of the many people

I had worked with over the past ten years would send me a letter like this. The letter was oozing with anger. *Whoever wrote this is almost out of control with anger*, I thought as I re-read the message. I knew from reading the accounts of various killings that occurred over the years that many of them happened when a person was violently angry, lost control of his senses, and did things he never otherwise would do. Anger is a powerful emotion, no question about it.

12
The Lathrops

The ringing phone in the outer office jerked me out of my malaise.

"Young man on the phone says he wants to talk to you and wonders if you'll come out to his place," said Gladys, who had taken the call.

I pushed the correct button on the phone and said, "Hello, this is Scott."

"My name is Don Lathrop. My wife and our two kids bought ten acres here in Ames County, and we want to start a vegetable business. Could you come out to our place and give us some tips?"

"Sure," I said, writing down his address on the notepad by my desk. "How about two o'clock this afternoon?"

I was once more thinking about my supervisor, who had been instructing me to make fewer farm calls and direct people to the various Extension websites where they could learn on their own without "wasting valuable agent time." I did refer people to the Extension's website when the questions seemed to have rather obvious answers, such as what's the average number of frost-free days in Ames County and to what extent the number of frost-free days has increased over the past few years with climate change. This information is readily available on the Internet. But that was not so easily answered if the person asking the question wanted to know what this information meant for his future farming operations. The answer to that question is not on the Internet because it requires weighing various pieces of information, doing considerable thinking about it and then making a judgment. This is where an educator can help and a county Extension agent can be of assistance.

At one-thirty, I climbed into my pickup, set the GPS to the address, and set out for the Lathrops' farm. I was rather looking forward to it. I enjoyed talking with people face-to-face. I remember what Otto Janson once told me. He had been the agricultural agent in this county for many years and was well respected, even though today's Extension administration would say he was not keeping up-to-date with the new communication technology that had exploded on the scene in the last twenty years.

"Sometimes you've got to talk to people by hand," Otto said. What he meant by that was talking to people face-to-face, without a telephone, computer, a smartphone, or some other piece of fancy electronics muddling the conversation.

"You've got to see the reaction to what you're saying to people in their eyes and what they are doing with their hands, not only listening to the words coming out their mouths. You've got to be able to 'read' people."

I've never forgotten Otto's words. In our haste as educators to latch onto every piece of electronics that has come down the pike, we sometimes forget that these are human beings listening to us. They have feelings. They have personal histories that often affect what we are trying to tell them. They are interested in making a living and improving their bottom lines, but their interests are broader than that—for most of them, anyway. I was looking forward to learning more about the Lathrop family, what brought them to Ames County, and even how they knew to call my office for help.

I parked my pickup in front of a rather forlorn-looking old farmhouse that badly needed paint. I spotted a late-model SUV parked under a big oak tree that had not yet begun to leaf out. I glanced over at what had once been a dairy barn, but part of the roof was missing, and the old barn was likely doomed, along with so many old dairy barns here in Ames County. A previous owner had put up a steel shed. It looked in reasonable shape. An old slatted corncrib was sagging and ready to tip; what had once been a granary was also on its last legs. As I walked to the house and stepped onto the kitchen porch, I wondered if the Lathrop family knew what they had gotten into.

I rapped on the kitchen door.

"Hi, I'm Scott Olson from the University Extension Office," I said when the door opened.

"I'm Jane, Jane Lathrop. So good of you to come out to our place." She stepped out on the porch. Jane was tall. She had a bright, pleasant smile. I'd guess she was in her late thirties. She wore new-looking bib overalls and was carrying a little girl, about a year old. A little blond-haired boy, maybe three, stuck his head out from behind his mother and then retreated again.

"These are our two kids. This is Constance. She'll be two years old next spring. And this little guy, the shy one, is Ben. Ben is three." Ben looked around his mother once more at me.

"Don is around somewhere."

I looked around and saw a tall, thin man emerge from the back of the metal shed. He, too, wore bib overalls. He smiled broadly when he approached and thrust out his hand to shake mine.

"You must be the county agent," he said.

"I'm Scott Olson, from the Extension Office in Willow River."

"So good of you to drive out here. Really appreciate it. Did Jane give you any background on what we are planning?" Don Lathrop looked to be in his early forties, trim and thin, mostly bald.

"Not yet," I said, smiling. "I just got here."

"Well come on in," he said. "House isn't much yet, but we've got plans to fix it up. We bought ten acres here, which included these old, tired buildings. We need lots of help. More than I thought we'd need."

Don proceeded to tell me that he had grown up in Waukesha and that his wife was from La Crosse. "Jane and I met when we attended Badger State University. Both of us are business majors."

"Business background should help you here on the farm," I offered.

"I hope so," chimed in Jane, who walked to the far side of the kitchen and put another stick of wood in the woodstove.

"Well, after we got married right out of college, we both got jobs in Milwaukee, and we did okay. Earned a lot of money. We thought we were living the good life." Don smiled when he said it.

I listened carefully as Don continued his story, one that I had heard several times in the past few years as more and more young families left the city for the country.

"Well, when the kids came along," Jane continued, "we weren't so sure we wanted them to grow up in the city. We did a lot of reading about country life and the challenges we might face, especially when we decided that we'd try to make a living growing vegetables."

"We both read I don't know how many books on gardening. But somehow, once we got here, it all ... well it all seemed overwhelming," said Don. "That's why I called you. Somebody in the office where I worked had grown up on a farm and said, 'If you got a farm question, call the county agent.' And that's what I did."

"It's really none of my business, but I must ask, how is your financial situation?" Both Jane and Don smiled at my question. More often I get a "that's really none of your business" look when I ask about finances. But finances become critical, especially if people plan to do something they haven't done before. I've seen too many young couples, not too different from the Lathrops, who have romantic ideas about making a living in the "wonderful country" and move back to the city disillusioned with the reality that they confronted.

"Once we decided we didn't want to work in big business for our entire careers, we started saving as much money as we could. And I think we did okay. We paid cash for these ten acres—I know we've got to put thousands into fixing up this old house—we've planned for that. And I'm smart enough to know that if we want to grow vegetables we'll have to buy some equipment, seeds, that sort of thing. I think we'll be good for at least two or three years, which should give us time to figure things out and get a little experience with vegetable growing."

"Well, one of the first things I suggest you do is get in touch with Jodi Henderson. Jodi is president of the Small-Acreage Farmers

Association. Jodi came out of Chicago. Let's see, it must be ten years ago now, and she and her husband, Bill, and their three kids have done quite well doing what I believe you are planning."

I tore off a piece of paper from the little notebook I always carry in my pocket, which includes a directory of people I often contact. I wrote down Jodi's phone number and email address and handed it to Jane.

I went on to explain how becoming a member of the Small-Acreage Farmers Association would not only provide them with ready access to the collective knowledge of the group, but I explained that the group ran the farmers' market in Willow River each summer.

I spent the next hour discussing everything from how to get their soil tested to what vegetable varieties do well on the sandy soils of Ames County. When I pushed back my chair to leave, Jane said, "You can't go yet. You've got to try some cookies that little Ben and I made this morning and have a cup of coffee."

For another half hour I ate chocolate chip cookies, drank coffee, and talked about the history of Willow River and Ames County. I had almost forgotten the threatening letters I'd recently received.

13
Will Curry

When I stepped into my car, my cell phone rang. It was Gladys at the office.

"Just got a call from Will Curry. He wants you to stop out at his place before you come back to the office."

"Did he say what he wanted?"

"Something about his cows not doing so well these days," Gladys said.

I had known Will Curry for about as long as I have been working in Ames County. Will was now in his eighties. He farmed 160 acres, the same land that his grandfather and father before him had operated. Will had a small dairy herd, maybe thirty-five cows, and farmed mostly like he did forty years ago. Whenever I held an Extension meeting that had anything to do with livestock or dairy farming, he sat in the front row, nodding his head in agreement with what I was saying. Some of what I said he practiced. A lot of it he didn't, especially if what I was saying flew in the face of what he wanted to do, knew how to do, and had always done. For instance, when several of the dairy farmers in the county expanded their dairy herds in the early 2000s, and today milk a thousand or more cows, he wouldn't do it. He figured he knew how to care for thirty-five cows, which should be enough to provide him with a reasonable living.

Will's farm is a showplace. The barn is painted a bright red, the farmhouse is painted white, and the rest of the buildings in the farmstead are in good repair. Will's wife, Rose, died ten years ago. Will told me once that in her memory he always kept a row of rose bushes growing alongside the house. If you wanted a picture of what a family farm of the sixties looked like, Will's was it.

For early May it was a warm day, the thermometer climbing into the mid-sixties. I parked my truck by the farmhouse and spotted Will sitting on his porch in his rocking chair. He smiled broadly when he saw me. Will's collie barked a couple of times and then ran over to me, its tail wagging. I bent down and petted the friendly dog.

"Thanks for stopping by, Scott," he said when he shook my hand.

"Nice day. See you got your cows out."

"Haven't got any pasture yet, but they deserve a day in the sunshine. Just look at those young heifers running around the yard and kicking up their heels. Always enjoy the young stock when I let them out in the spring. Nothing seems to enjoy spring weather as much as young stock cooped up in the barn all winter."

"Gladys said you had a problem you wanted to talk about?"

"Cows have really dropped off on their production the last month. I'm trying to figure out what I'm doing wrong," Will said as he slowly got up from his rocking chair.

"Let's walk over to the barnyard and have you give them a look over. Maybe you can see something that I've missed."

Will and I walked over to the barnyard. We both leaned on the neat white board fence that surrounded the enclosure.

"Cows are a little thin," I said after looking from one to another. "Other than that, they seem okay. It's been a long winter. Once they are out on pasture, I'm sure they'll put on a little weight. Too much weight on a cow isn't good either, but you know that. A fat cow is generally not a good producer."

"Scott, it'll be mid-month or later the way the weather has been before my cow pasture is gonna amount to anything."

"So what are you feeding now?"

We walked into the barn, and I picked up some alfalfa hay that was in the manger in front of where the cows stood when they were in the barn.

"Hay looks like mostly stems. Not many leaves on it," I said.

"It's all I've got left to feed. Hate to have to buy hay with pasture season coming up."

"Well, I think the quality of your hay is the problem, Will. Cows don't produce much milk with poor quality hay."

"I should know that, shouldn't I? You've said it often enough at your meetings."

"Do you remember when you cut this hay?"

"I do. Lots going on last June when I should have been haying. Lots going on, and I didn't get it cut until the first week in July. You think that's the problem?"

"That's the problem, Will. Poor hay, poor production."

After a bit more discussion about the nutritional needs of dairy cows—what I'm sure Will already knew—I shook his hand, patted his big collie on the head, and climbed back in my pickup.

As I drove back toward the office, I thought about my afternoon in the country and how, within a couple of hours, I had seen firsthand how agriculture had been in Ames County when I talked with Will Curry and got a glimpse of what the future of agriculture was beginning to look like after my visit with the Lathrop family.

I also reaffirmed my belief that as long as I could, I would try and find some time to talk with people face-to-face on their farms. The new digital information revolution may be an aid to teaching, but it can never replace talking with people, seeing their situation, and getting a feel for their questions and problems in addition to hearing them talk about their challenges.

I stopped in Overlook Park, as I often did on my return to my office in Willow River. I remembered doing this when I saw Willow River for the first time, the day I was interviewed for the Extension agent position. Willow River looked the same. Ames Lake looked the same. But as some wag once said: "Looks can be deceiving."

Underneath this quiet scene, anxiety, fear, and even a bit of hatred bubbled to the surface from time to time. The people of Ames County were on edge. Many no longer talked with each other, even families torn apart as people sided with what they called the "big farmer movement" or a "return to the family farm" group. Big against small. Environmentalists were becoming increasingly strident and active, sometimes well-informed and sometimes not.

Here I was, right in the middle of this anger and fear, often fueled by misinformation or no information at all, as people too often rely on opinion and hearsay to reach the conclusions that they do.

I started the pickup, drove to the courthouse, and parked in the spot with the faded little sign: "Reserved for County Agent."

14
Water Problems

"Scott, you just missed a call from Dan Lathrop," Gladys said when I returned to the office. I have my own cell phone, but Gladys handles all of my appointments.

"Did he say what he wanted?"

"No, but he said it was important."

I looked up Lathrop's number and punched in the numbers.

"This is Scott," I said when I heard Lathrop's voice. "What can I do for you?"

"We've got a problem—a big problem," he said.

I had just been out to their farm, and everything seemed in order. Unlike some of the city folks who moved out to Ames County to take up "farming," he and his wife appeared to have done their homework and were well aware of the challenges they faced on their new property.

"We just got some bad news in the mail," Lathrop continued. "We sent a water sample from our well to Madison to be tested. Just got the results back, and our well water exceeds the safety standards for bacteria and nitrates. We can't drink the water is the bottom line."

"I am sorry to hear that," I said; however, I thought, *I'm not surprised. I knew about the big dairy farm that had been expanding in their neighborhood. They now milked six thousand cows and spread their manure on nearby farm fields.*

"What are we going to do?" Lathrop asked. "We're buying drinking water. I'm really afraid for my kids. Had we known our water was bad, we probably wouldn't have bought this place. The realtor said the water was fine when I asked."

"I know this is not what you want to hear, Don, but several landowners in your part of the county have reported contaminated wells, believed to be caused by manure seeping into the aquifer and elevating the levels of nitrogen and bacteria in the water."

"What can we do?"

"You can check with a well driller and drill a deeper well. And, of course, do what you have been doing: buy drinking water," I said.

"Thanks, Scott. I'll see what we can do."

I could tell from his tone of voice that he wasn't too happy with my suggestions. Drilling a new, deeper well would be costly, and I knew the Lathrops had all of their current and future expenses carefully planned, and it didn't include drilling a new well.

One more problem to add to Ames County's many challenges. Realtors should make sure water is tested before there is a sale. I knew of the problems that people in Kewaunee County faced with manure contamination of well water, and I guess I was naïve in not believing the same problems would one day come to Ames County, as we now had several dairy herds with more than one thousand cows. It was likely to become a problem in other areas of the state as well. I'd read some recent DNR figures that said that Wisconsin dairy farms with more than five hundred cows had grown by more than 150 percent in the last ten years. And in the country as a whole, the number of dairy operations with two thousand cows and more had grown faster than those of any other size.

I also remember reading that a dairy operation of two thousand cows produces more than 240,000 pounds of manure daily, which amounts to nearly ninety million pounds a year. Now I had one more problem to add to the list for the planning council to contend with. Once the word got out that manure was contaminating well water in the community where the Lathrops lived, all hell would break loose.

When Jill Varsac and CFTF hear about this, the world will soon know about it. And our office will be caught right in the middle, along with the Department of Natural Resources.

Thoughts of the two threatening letters seemed to bubble to the top of my thinking almost every waking hour and sometimes, too many times, in the middle of the night. And now, I couldn't help but think of the young couple, the Lathrops, who moved to Ames County and had asked for my help. I always felt good when I was able to provide it. But now they've got a new problem that I've got to start working on.

As I was thinking about this, Gladys knocked quietly on my door and entered.

"You'll want to read this," Gladys said as she handed me the recent issue of the *Ames County Gazette*.

I glanced at the clock; it read 5:30, well past closing time for the office. One thing I learned about Gladys when I began working in this office was that she didn't leave for the day until she finished the work that she wanted to complete. She knew that Sarah and I often worked all day in the office and half the evening at one meeting or another. Gladys certainly didn't need to work as many hours a week as we did, but I appreciated her work ethic, and I told her so periodically.

I unfolded the new issue of the *Gazette*, and on the front page I read:

"Winter Lake Property Owners Meet: Irate Over Dropping Water Levels"

More than fifty people turned out for the annual meeting of the Winter Lake Property Owners Association. Winter Lake is located in western Ames County.

Almost immediately the discussion turned to the dramatic drop of the lake level during the past ten years. Several people said that in front of their cabins, where there had been water, it now looked like an overgrown cow pasture. Everyone was asking why was this happening? Was it part of a natural water cycle, as everyone knew that the lake was a water-table lake with neither an inlet nor an outlet. Would the lake soon be returning to its early level? Was there another cause for the severe drop in the water level, and if so, what or who could be blamed?

George Emerson, the group's attorney and a property owner on the lake, had been asked at a previous meeting to look into the reasons for the rapid drop in the lake level. Emerson shared what he had learned. He said, "We all know that as recently as ten years ago, our lake was, on average, fifteen feet deep and as deep as twenty-five feet in several places. We all remember the wonderful black bass many of us caught and the fun our kids had water-skiing. What we have left, as you all know, is a pond. The fish are gone—winter killed them because the lake level is so low. And no one would think of water-skiing on what's left of our once wonderful lake.

"I believe I have the answer. In the 1960s this area in central Wisconsin had about 100 high-capacity wells that farmers used for irrigating their crops. Today that number has increased to more than 3,000 wells. Several high-capacity wells are located within a mile of our lake. These wells can pump as many as 100,000 gallons of water a day, which is about the amount of water a typical family with showers, dishwashing, and lawn sprinkling would use in a year."

The group was quick to blame the farmers in the area for their lake's demise. Attorney Emerson said the issue was a bit more complicated than merely blaming the farmers or even suing nearby vegetable farmers using high-capacity wells. The group appointed a four-person committee, with George Emerson as chair, to explore steps the group could take to try and restore the level of Winter Lake.

I read the piece a second time, sat back in my chair, and ran my hand through my hair. *What else do we need?* I thought. The big commercial farmers are fed up with the small-acreage farmers, the small-acreage farmers believe the big farmers are ruining the environment, big dairy farmers are contaminating well water, and now the cabin owners want to go after the vegetable farmers who irrigate—to say nothing about an increasing number of city folk who think farmers, no matter large or small, are one of the country's biggest problems.

I set the newspaper aside and walked into the now-dark outer office—Gladys had left. I locked the office door and drove over to Sarah's place. I had spent a night or two at Sarah's cabin for quite some time. I assumed most people knew this and didn't say anything. Sarah and I had discussed getting married, but we each thought it best to wait until some of the ruckus in Ames County had settled down and didn't require so much of our time.

"How about a big salad for each of us tonight," Sarah said when I opened the door and entered the kitchen. "Sounds like you had a busy day, from what Gladys said when I asked where you were."

"It was a great day, mostly," I said. She raised her eyes with the word *mostly*, waiting for my story. I told her about the young couple who had recently moved onto an old, abandoned farm in the western part of the county and planned to take up vegetable growing. And I mentioned the phone call about their well water. I told her about my visit to Will Curry's place and how he was probably just lonely and wanted to chat for a bit. I told Sarah that Will knew as much about feeding cows and what made for good alfalfa hay as I did.

I reminded her of the recent news article in the *Gazette* asking retired farmers to send in stories of what farming was like fifty-plus years ago. I wanted to mention that it was her old boyfriend's idea to do that, but I thought better of it. Sarah did not want to be teased about her old flame.

Sarah said, "How would it be if I asked some of the older Homemaker members to talk about what home life on the farm was like in the early days? I'd guess we'd get several responses."

"Great idea. Do it."

"Excuse me a second," Sarah said as she retreated to the kitchen.

She was soon back with a bottle of wine and a couple of glasses. She handed the opener to me. With the bottle open, I poured merlot into her glass and then mine.

"Everything had been going so well and then, well, guess what happened?"

"I can't imagine," Sarah said, remembering the threatening letter I had recently received. I told Sarah about the article on the front page of the *Gazette* that Gladys saved for me.

"That article has opened up another bag of worms," I said.

"How so?" Sarah began filling big bowls with lettuce, some shredded Swiss cheese, and some tomatoes that she had gotten from one of our small-acreage farmers who raised tomatoes in a greenhouse.

"Well, this bunch of lake cabin owners—most of them from Milwaukee and Chicago—are mad as hell about the Winter Lake level dropping to the point that it is now merely a pond. At least that's what the article said."

"Someone mentioned that to me the other day as well," Sarah said, appearing unsurprised at what I had just said.

"Well, this group has an attorney; his name is Emerson. He is heading up a committee to do something about the problem. They are blaming the big vegetable farmers and their high-capacity wells for drying up their lake. He's got a point."

"Tell you what, Scott, let's enjoy dinner, let's enjoy the evening, and tomorrow we can begin worrying once more about who's mad at whom and what can be done about it."

15

Winter Lake

I drove slowly from Sarah's place toward the office. It was a beautiful morning. The tulips and daffodils were up and showing off their reds and yellows and purples. And the lawns in Willow River were beginning to green up. A bright sun reflected off the waters of Ames Lake, where Sarah's little cabin was located. At least Ames Lake's level hadn't dropped. It was hard to explain to people that lakes, like Ames Lake, have a river running in and out of it and have a different hydrology than the little water-table lakes in the western part of the county that have neither inlets nor outlets and are dependent on the aquifer beneath them for their supply of water.

I was at my desk by eight o'clock, feeling rested and with a clear mind. Gladys had arrived in the office by seven-thirty and had the coffee pot going, as has been her practice for as long as I had known her.

"Ready for a cup of coffee?" Gladys said after I hung up my coat and cap and settled into my chair. The copy of the *Gazette* with the troubling article was on the corner of the desk where I had left it.

She came into the office with a steaming cup of freshly brewed coffee in a big mug with "County Agent" on it. "So, what's on your schedule today—catching up on your reports?" She said this with a big smile because she knew how much I hated writing reports.

"I wanna drive out to Winter Lake and have a look at it myself—see how bad the situation really is. Give me a jingle on my cellphone if something important comes up."

Winter Lake was about fifteen miles west of Willow River, in the midst of the county's big, irrigated vegetable growing area. As I was driving to Winter Lake, I thought about the history of this huge, flat area. It had once been a glacial lake when the last glacier melted and left this area some ten thousand years ago. The lake was still there in many respects but now a few feet below the sandy surface. For many years, especially from the 1930s until the 1950s, these thousands of sandy acres were declared worthless for farming because the sandy soil was so droughty. But with the development of lightweight aluminum during World War II, which led to aluminum irrigation pipes, now water for potatoes and other vegetable crops became available, and what had once been worthless farmland was transformed into one of Wisconsin's premier vegetable growing areas. And all because of irrigation water.

As I drove along, I saw several farmers in their fields, attending to irrigation equipment where long rows of potatoes extended as far as I could see. The huge irrigation sweeps stood quietly. If the spring rains were sparse, farmers turned on the irrigation sweeps to make sure the potatoes grew well.

Amid the fast, flat, vegetable growing area, tucked in a little valley that had formed when the glacier melted, is Winter Lake, once sixty acres. I spotted the sign "Winter Lake County Park" and drove down the narrow, now seldom-used dirt road that led to the park and access to the lake.

I parked my truck and walked to the shore, surprised to see a pond of maybe five acres, with tall grass growing where once there was lake water. I remember when I was assistant county agent, and then county agent Otto Janson and I went fishing here several times each summer. We caught lots of fish, including big perch and even bigger black bass. Otto was a good fisherman; he'd catch two or three fish to my one. But as I've long known, fishing is much more than catching fish. I remember those conversations I had with Otto, especially the county agent stories from the early days. He shared stories about when he worked as a young assistant county agent in Marinette County. He told me about the early Extension agents in that county who gave dynamite to local farmers to blow up stumps in their fields. The stumps were left following the great logging era of the late 1800s and early 1900s. He talked about how those early agents gave demonstrations on how to use dynamite. It was dangerous work because one never knew if the dynamite was going to explode. He told farmers to never approach a stump with a stick of dynamite under it to check why it didn't go off. Too often the dynamite blew up in the farmer's face, blowing him and the stump into little pieces and leaving behind a widow and a house full of little kids to farm the dreary acres.

We talked about how county Extension work had changed over the years, but the dreaded reports remained. He told me when I was first hired to concentrate on the people. He often said, "The people come first. The reports can come later." I have tried to follow his advice and have occasionally gotten into trouble when my reports were late.

I remember saying to him one time, "Otto, some days the work seems to never get done. The phone calls pile up. There's a bunch of people who want me out on their farms."

Once again, I've never forgotten Otto's words: "Do the best you can with what you've got." I've been trying to do that, but some days I wonder if my best is not good enough for what people expect of me.

As I sat at a picnic table in Winter Lake Park, I thought of those early days and remembered how overwhelmed I often felt. I recall working every day and every night for fifteen days. And still there was more work to do. It was Otto who said I'd better learn when to say yes and when to say no to requests. "You can't do everything," he said. And how right he was.

What I don't remember from those early days here as an Extension agent is the anger many people feel today. In those early days, there was always some friendly kidding among farmers, but nothing like the rancor I see today between the big commercial dairy and vegetable growers and the small-acreage farmers. And it's only been during the last half dozen years or so, since the Eagle Party has gained more seats in the national and state government, that I've been hearing the cry to cut the number of government workers and eliminate tax-supported programs. "Got way too many people living off the backs of hardworking taxpayers" is a comment I seldom heard until recently.

Of course, I'm biased, but those who want to eliminate Extension workers, like myself, may not realize that we are a direct tie to the research available from Badger State University. Besides, we try our best to be impartial and not take sides in the issues that seem to bubble up more every year. I know this may sound arrogant, but I believe Extension agents want to bring people together, help them understand each other, provide factual, research-based information for the discussion, and not rush to judge their fellow human beings based on hearsay, emotion, and inaccurate information.

Of course, I can't get the threatening letters I've recently received out of my mind. Never before has anyone threatened me. There have been disagreements. Some people have not liked the advice that I've given and have even discounted the researched information I've provided. But these threatening letters have been an exception.

I looked across Winter Lake and saw a big, beautiful log house that likely cost the owner a million dollars to build. I wonder who owned it, and I wonder what he thought about the declining water level of Winter Lake. I would soon find out.

16
Invitation to a Meeting

It was noon when I returned to Willow River. I decided to stop for lunch at the Country Cooking Restaurant, the same one where I ate when I first drove into town some ten years ago, and where I eat lunch several times a week. About all that changed since I first ate there was the ownership and the help.

"What can I get for you, Scott," a perky young waitress with a ponytail said as I found a place in the back.

"Hi, Trudy. What's your special today?" I knew Trudy Wilson when she was an active 4-H member in our county 4-H program. Her parents moved to Willow River from Chicago and bought this little restaurant.

"Barbeque short ribs," Trudy said. "And they're pretty good, too. Come with mashed potatoes and green beans."

"Sounds good to me." I glanced around the room, checking to see who I might know. I spotted Police Chief Wilkins sitting with one of his deputies on the other side of the room. When I finished eating, I stopped by his table.

"How you doing, Scott?" Wilkins said. "You know Officer Arnold, don't you?"

"I do, how are you, Ann?"

"I'm doing okay," she said. Ann Arnold had been on the force only a year and had already gained the respect of the citizens of Willow River. She made news shortly after she was hired when she stopped the mayor for going forty miles an hour in a twenty-five mile-per-hour speed zone. The mayor has been kidded about that encounter ever since.

"I was wondering if you'd gotten any information about the hate letters?"

"Nothing yet. I've turned the investigation over to Ann, and she's following up with the crime lab in Madison. I suspect it'll be a while before we hear."

"Any more problems like that?" the chief asked.

"Not so far. Hard not to think about the letters, though."

"I know how you feel. A couple years ago I arrested this fellow for drug dealing, and he said when he got out of prison, he'd shoot me. He's still in prison, and I hope he stays there. And that's not the only threat I've gotten. Seems to go with the territory."

I drove the short distance from the restaurant to my office in the courthouse, wondering if those hate letters were a fluke, somebody trying to let off steam. I hoped so.

"Several phone calls," Gladys said when I entered the office. "Better call George Emerson. He's the attorney who lives out on Winter Lake and was quoted in the paper."

I wondered what Emerson wanted as I punched his number into my phone.

"George Emerson here," I heard after three rings.

"This is Scott Olson from the Extension Office. I believe you called."

"Yes, I did. I'm president of the Winter Lake Property Owners Association. You know where Winter Lake is, I assume."

"I do. I used to fish there. What can I do for you?"

"You probably saw the piece in the paper about the declining lake levels on our lake?"

"Yes, I saw the article." I wondered what Attorney Emerson wanted.

"You work with Ames County farmers, I believe. Is that right?"

"Yes, that's right," I answered. I went on to explain that I was employed by both Badger State University as well as Ames County, and I, as an educator, had a responsibility to work with all of the people in Ames County. I explained that the people living in rural communities were one of the primary groups I work with.

"Well, I was wondering if you would be available to meet with a small committee that's looking into why our lake level has dropped so much in the past few years."

"Sure," I said, hoping my voice didn't sound defensive because I knew that these lake owners blamed the vegetable farmers and their irrigation systems for drawing down the level of their lake. "Where and when?"

"How about next Wednesday at two in the afternoon at my home on the lake?" He gave me the address, which I wrote down. I immediately wondered if his was the big, million-dollar home I had seen when I was out there a few days ago.

"That will work. Anything in particular you want from me?"

"We're all pretty upset about what's happening to our beautiful lake. We want your take on what's going on and what we can do about it."

"See you next Wednesday," I said. *One more piece of the anger puzzle in Ames County. Let's see, we've got the small-acreage farmers mad at the big commercial farmers. Some of the commercial farmers make fun of the small-acreage farmers, especially those who farm organically. Then there's the Citizens for the Future group that seems to be mad at all the farmers, and now we've got lake owners mad at the large vegetable growers and their irrigation systems. What a mess. Everybody is shouting at each other and nobody is listening.*

17
Contentious Meeting

I drove slowly out to Winter Lake, taking a different route than the other day. I drove by several small-acreage farmers. I'd met most of them. They were busy in their gardens, setting out tomato plants, planting sweet corn seeds, setting pepper plants. I could see rows of lettuce and radishes already up and growing well. When I drove over the little ridge that marked the terminal moraine, where the glacier stopped, I looked across what had been the vast expanse of Glacial Lake Wisconsin. I saw enormous tractors working in the fields. I thought about how different this area must have looked back in the 1950s before farmers in this part of the county knew about deep-well irrigation pumps and the enormous irrigation sweeps that now stood off to the side of fields five hundred acres or more in size.

I remember talking with some of the old-timers who told me about how they grew up in this area. They told me about how their families farmed 160 acres in the 1950s and 1960s. They milked fifteen or twenty cows and grew twenty acres of corn, as many acres of oats, and sometimes twenty acres of potatoes as a cash crop, along with an acre of cucumbers for the kids to pick in the summer and make a little extra money. They told me about the neat farmsteads, the barns and the granaries, and the farmhouses on each of these farms. Some of the farmsteads remain, but not many. The buildings were torn down or burned when the land was bought out by neighbors and consolidated into the big land holdings we see today. They told me how much they depended on the rain, and if the rains didn't come regularly, their crops suffered, their yields dropped, and they struggled to make it through the year.

I knew I would soon be reading stories about those years on the farm, when the stories began arriving in the *Gazette's* office, as I knew they would. Old-timers like to tell their stories. I hoped people would read them and perhaps learn something from them. I didn't know if it would happen, but I can always hope.

I followed the directions I had gotten, and I had guessed correctly. The meeting would be at the big house I had seen the other day when I came out to Winter Lake to check on the lake level. I parked my pickup alongside a black Cadillac Escalade. I didn't see many vehicles like this in Ames County.

I walked up to the door and pushed the doorbell button.

"I'm Scott Olson," I said.

A tall, middle-aged man with a closely cropped white beard said, "Thanks for coming. I'm George Emerson. I talked with you on the phone. The other lake owners are in the other room." He shook my hand. He had a firm handshake to go along with the confident look on his face and his dark, rather penetrating eyes.

I have been in many situations like this over the years, when people were angry about something, and they called me in to help make things better—or at least that's what they believed when they invited me. On the surface, this appeared to be one of those situations.

"This is the Ames County agricultural agent," Emerson said. I stood beside him as he introduced the other people sitting around the big oak table that sat in front of an enormous fieldstone fireplace.

"This good-looking fellow is Mike Braun," Emerson said, smiling. "Mike is from Chicago, where he worked for many years in manufacturing."

"Hello," said Braun. No smile. Mostly a frown on a deeply wrinkled face. I would take him to be in his early fifties. He looked to be in good physical shape.

"And this is Lisa Lenfeld. She's a retired teacher from Milwaukee and has the place next door to mine."

"Very nice to meet you," said Lisa. "Several of my nieces and nephews are in 4-H, so I know a little bit about what your office does."

"And finally, this is Curtis Callahan. Curt is a realtor who mostly lives and works in Oshkosh, but he spends as much time as he can here on Winter Lake."

"Thanks for coming," said Callahan. "I hope you can help us with the problem that is pretty obvious for all to see."

"I'll help if I can," I said, trying not to sound defensive. Curtis had a friendly look about him. He was tall, thin, and had graying hair. He was probably in his late forties.

"Here, Scott, why don't you sit at the end of the table?" Emerson said, pulling back a huge, high-backed chair that matched the oak table.

I sat down, trying to make myself comfortable as everyone looked in my direction, hoping that I might possess some magic to return the level of their lake to what it was twenty years ago.

"Scott, I think you know why we asked you to attend our meeting. I'll be blunt; I hope you don't mind."

"Go ahead," I said, not knowing exactly what he was going to say.

"We know that as Ames County agricultural agent you represent the farmers here in Ames County. Am I right about that?"

"Well, I don't represent the farmers in this county. I am here to share research findings from the university with farmers and whoever finds the information useful. My job is that of an educator." I looked toward Lisa Lenfeld for some sort of reaction. I got none. "You'll recall when we talked on the phone, I mentioned our Extension Office has the responsibility of working with everyone in the county, with a special emphasis on agriculture and those people related to farming."

"But you know many of the farmers here in Ames County, right?" said Emerson.

"Yes, I do," I proudly said. "I've been working here for ten years, and yes, I've met, and I hope, helped a lot of farmers."

"So, are you the guy that showed these big vegetable growers with those damn irrigation outfits how to dry up our lake?" piped up Mike Braun. His voice was filled with anger.

"I wouldn't say it quite that way," I said, wondering where this exchange was going.

"Well how would you say it? You work with farmers. You said that. They use our water, and our lake dries up. My wife and I retired here. We spent all of our savings on that little house you see across the lake—what had once been a lake, and now what? No lake. And the value of our property is about half. Half of my savings gone."

Emerson interrupted, "Mike, I think we know how you feel. My place isn't worth nearly as much as it was when Winter Lake was lapping at the shore just down the hill from where we are sitting. But we asked Scott to meet with us and offer some suggestions as to what we might do about our situation."

I looked at Mike Braun, who sat across from me at the table. His face was red, and the muscles in his neck were throbbing.

"Sorry, George, but what I've got to say needs sayin'," said Braun. "Sounds like this here government guy is the one who taught these damn irrigatin' farmers how to do it, how to drain the water out of our lake. I grew up hatin' government people, and this here county agent government guy is no different from any of the other government guys I've come across over the years. You can't trust any of 'em. They got these cushy jobs with all kinds of benefits. And who pays their salaries? We do. The people who pay taxes. Those of us who have worked hard all our lives. Our tax dollars go to these government guys who sit in fancy offices, and they end up screwin' us, just like this guy has done."

As I listened to this tirade, which was the first time I had heard it said to me personally, I wondered if maybe this was the guy who wrote the threatening letters to me. He sure sounded like a candidate.

"Calm down, Mike," said Emerson, reaching over and putting his hand on Mike Braun's arm. He shrugged it off. "Angry words won't solve our problem."

"Then what in the hell will? Tell me that. Somebody's gotta speak up. Look at you, every one of you. Just sitting there, sitting on your hands, letting this damn government guy drain our lake and ruin our lives," said Braun as he made a sweeping motion with his arm.

"Well, this damn meeting is goin' nowhere. I've got better things to do." Braun pushed back on his chair, which tipped over with a loud bang. "I'm gettin' the hell out of here. Let me know if you figure somethin' out." He stomped toward the door, opened it, and slammed it shut.

Those left sitting around the table sat quietly for a few moments, all looking toward the door from which their angry neighbor had just left.

Emerson let out his breath and said, "That's a side of Mike I haven't seen before. Sorry you had to hear all of that, Scott. It was my idea to ask you to our meeting. I'm sure Mike will remind me of that when he cools off, and we can talk."

After Braun left the meeting, I talked about how the Department of Natural Resources provided permits to farmers with deep-well irrigation systems.

"You should get in touch with Jill Varsac," I suggested. I told them about her environmental group and the work that they were doing. I offered this reluctantly, as Varsac's approach often ruffled more feathers than it soothed. But, although I would never say this out loud, feathers sometimes need a bit of ruffling to get people's attention.

A couple of the lake owners said they knew about her group. I then said, "Your group should work out a strategy that includes having a frank talk with DNR representatives, and if that doesn't seem to work, invite your state senator and assembly representative to one of your meetings. Show them your lake. Share with them the research information that you have."

Back in my office later that afternoon, I tried to think through the meeting I'd had with the Winter Lake residents. Three of them seemed sincere about learning more about what they could do, but the meeting took a sour turn almost before it started with Mike Braun's tirade against government workers. This was the first time I had been lumped together with all government workers, which, let me see, would include the FBI, the military, the people who run the Social Security offices, the police officers, firefighters, teachers—we are all government workers. I wonder if Braun has ever thought about that. I'm guessing that he is a card-carrying member of the Eagle Party and has bought into the party's harangues about how the government is ruining the country.

The phone rang as I was trying to think of what I might do to help this group.

"This is Scott."

"George Emerson. I wanted to call and apologize once more for what happened at our meeting. Mike's words were uncalled for. I knew he had a bit of a temper, but, well, I thought he'd know enough to carry on a civil conversation. I was obviously wrong."

"Thanks, George. Apology accepted. I know these are tough times, and a lot of people are on edge. I guess I was just somebody handy that Mike could go after."

"Apparently so. I'll try to follow up with your suggestions. Getting in touch with Jill Varsac and the CFTF group is a good idea. I've heard of the group, and if I remember correctly, they have a reputation for challenging anything and everything that seems to harm the environment. I'm curious if they'll want to include the dropping of lake levels on their agenda."

"They likely already have," I said, having remembered reading somewhere about the group's concern for what's happening to the state's groundwater.

"Can we keep in touch?" George asked.

"Sure, anyway I can help, just let me know. Oh, you might want to have a beer with your neighbor, Mike. He seems to have a lot he wants to get off his chest."

"I just might do that. But I think I'll wait a few days. Give him a chance to cool off. I've seen a lot of angry people in my work, but

Mike is right up there near the top. Angry people sometimes do weird things," George said.

"One other thing. Did you see the piece in the *Ames County Gazette* about the Agricultural Planning Council that we've recently organized?" I asked.

"I did see it."

"Would you have any interest in being a member of the group—lake property owners, as you well know, have a considerable relationship to farming."

"As we well know," said George. "Sure. When's your next meeting?"

I checked my calendar to make sure I was remembering correctly, "It's next week, Wednesday."

"I'll try and be there," Emerson said. We've got to do something about what's happening to the lake levels in this part of Ames County."

"Well, thanks again for your call. Much appreciated, and see you next week," I said as I hung up.

Now I was back thinking about Mike Braun. In my mind, he was a strong candidate for the source of the hate mail I've received. I wondered if George Emerson could cool him off a bit. Emerson seemed like a reasonable fellow. If anyone could talk with Braun, it would seem his attorney neighbor could do it.

18
Scott and Sarah

That evening at Sarah's place, I shared with her what happened at the Winter Lake meeting.

"So much anger these days. It seems everybody is mad at somebody," Sarah said. "Did you call the sheriff and tell him what happened?"

I said that I hadn't done that, and Braun really hadn't threatened any harm—I didn't think so anyway. "I really don't want the world to know that there's a group of people who want government workers to go away. That might just encourage those who haven't thought about it to join that bunch of government haters."

"Scott," Sarah said, taking both of my hands in hers and looking into my eyes. "Why don't we get married and leave this place? Go somewhere else and start all over again. You could be an agricultural consultant in one of these big ag firms; they'd give you a job in a minute and with probably twice the salary. And I could start a little restaurant that serves fresh food and offers local crafts and books for sale."

"Oh, Sarah," I said. "I'm so sorry to put you through all this. I really am. This is my problem, not yours."

"Scott, it's my problem, too." She began crying. "I'm not worried about losing my job. I'm worried about losing you. I don't know what

I'd do if I lost you."

"Oh, Sarah," I said, brushing away a tear from her face. "I wish I knew what to do. Ames County needs me, needs somebody to try and bring the county back together again."

"Let Ames County find somebody else to do it. I'm not so sure these various groups want to come together. They seem to enjoy jabbing at each other, calling each other names, trying to put each other down."

"I can't quit now, Sarah. Our new Agricultural Planning Council meets again next week. I think that group can make a difference."

"You really think so? Some of those people have agendas that won't budge. They believe compromise is a dirty word. They're on the council to move their agendas along."

"But I've got to try. Somebody's got to try. Somehow, we've got to help people realize that just because someone thinks and acts differently than they do, they shouldn't be hated. There's just too much of 'I'm right, and you're wrong, and I'm gonna make sure that you know it' going around."

"Scott, do you realize that you're gonna be right in the middle of these battling groups? You will be a convenient target—you already are. Those damn letters. I keep thinking about those letters, Scott. Somebody is already out to get you."

"Looks that way, Sarah. But what can I do? I remember my dad saying that life is filled with hills to climb. This surely is one of those hills, maybe even a mountain."

19
Portage Meeting

Sitting at my desk the following morning, I couldn't help moving my mind off what Sarah had said last night. This was the first time she had talked about marriage. I also thought a lot about marrying Sarah. She said she couldn't bear to lose me. Well, I could say the same. Without Sarah I don't know how I could face what I'm facing now.

I heard a quiet knock on my door. It was Gladys.

"Remember you've got a district meeting in Portage today, and don't forget, the meeting of the Agricultural Planning Council is set for Wednesday," she said.

"Thank you." I am so fortunate to have two women in my life who make things easier. One makes sure I keep to my schedule, and the other makes sure I maintain my sanity.

Sarah and I always rode together to the district Extension meetings held every couple of months for all Extension agents working in the southern Wisconsin Extension District. We meet at the Columbia County Courthouse in Portage. When I first started working for the Extension, the agents in the southern district nearly filled the room, but with budget cuts over the past several years, the room is only about half full, and many of these are new people who have replaced those who feared their jobs might be cut next and took early retirement or found other jobs.

Sarah and I said little as I drove my pickup along the interstate to Portage, about fifty miles from Willow River. I didn't bring up the previous night's discussion, as much as I wanted to. I wanted and should have told Sarah last evening how much I loved her and wanted to marry her. But I grew up in a family where words like *love* were seldom used. My dad said often: "Let your actions speak louder than your words." Saying "love" is surely an exception to that rule, but I haven't learned to say it. I hope Sarah knows I love her as much as she loves me.

I was thinking all these thoughts as we drove along on such a beautiful June day, one of those more than beautiful spring days in Wisconsin with green grass everywhere and the corn crop showing its first leaves in the fields we passed.

I parked the pickup in the courthouse parking lot, and Sarah and I joined our fellow agents in a big meeting room. Our district supervisor, Ben Ruskie, was fiddling with a computer projector, indicating that we once more would be subjected to one of Ben's PowerPoint presentations. Ben, as usual, was dressed in a three-piece suit with a bright red tie—almost matching his usual red face.

The meeting started promptly at nine o'clock. One thing about Ben Ruskie was that he was always on time, started meetings on time, and expected everyone else to be on time. "Rules are rules," he said. "And that means being on time." He has a point. I've wasted a lot of time in my career waiting for someone to show up at an indicated time, and then they were late. Most times, these latecomers didn't even offer an excuse, belonging to that group that used a specified start time only as a guide, not an absolute.

A big red, vastly enlarged dollar sign appeared on the screen. It alternately flashed from a brighter red to a dimmer red, but it kept flashing as Ruskie began talking.

"First, some budget information," he began, riffling through a stack of notes in front of him. He adjusted his glasses. We all disliked hearing about budgets, which can be and often is the most boring subject on earth, especially if you are an action person who believes someone else should look after your budget so you can do what needs doing without worrying too much about the cost.

But with the budget cuts over the past several years, we've all learned to pay attention. Ruskie didn't need to show a flashing dollar sign on the screen to do that.

"Since the Eagle Party has gained more power, we likely can expect fewer dollars coming to the Extension from the United States Department of Agriculture," Ruskie began. We all knew that about a third of our budgets came from the federal government, another third were state dollars, and the final third came from the counties where we work.

"And you are well aware that the Eagle Party mostly controls our state government these days. And, if you haven't already noticed," Ruskie said, pausing for emphasis, "the Eagle Party has a strong anti-government worker segment in the party. Some of you have no doubt been confronted with one of these anti-government people."

I wanted to hold up my hand and tell everyone what had been happening to me lately, the two threatening letters that I'd gotten, and the fellow going off at me during the Winter Lake meeting. But I thought it better to keep this to myself. I had shared some of this with Ruskie. I was glad he chose not to use me as an example of what this anti-government group was doing in Ames County.

"Anyway," Ruskie continued, "expect more budget cuts this next year. I don't have numbers yet, but the signs are not good."

What a way to enhance employee morale, I thought. Talk like this, and all the good Extension agents will bail out as soon as they can find other jobs.

"Given that rather gloomy report," Ruskie said, "here are some ideas for dealing with limited budgets, or as I might say, making every dollar do two dollars' worth of programming." He smiled when he said it, believing, I'm sure, that he just coined the most profound budget slogan ever.

A new illustration appeared on the screen. It was one of a laptop computer with lines leading from it to bubbles in which were written "New Idea," "Research Finding," "Badger Facts," and "Your Questions

Answered."

"We must learn to use the new technology we have available. We must learn to use our computers and the Internet in ways we haven't yet discovered," he said, raising his voice for emphasis.

"The Internet will be the way that one budget dollar can do the work of two," he said, coming back to his earlier slogan. He smiled when he said it.

"No more farm and home visits. They are too costly and time consuming. The only meetings should be those with large groups, where you can do technology transfer—sharing Badger State research findings in the most efficient way."

I wanted to hold up my hand and share with the group information about the new planning council we had just organized in Ames County, as a way to bring opposing groups together for better understanding. I'm glad I didn't because the next thing Ruskie said disturbed me and helped me understand why I didn't like him and considered his ideas one sure way of eventually destroying Extension.

"Remember, we are educators," Ruskie said, again adjusting his glasses and finding his place in his notes. On the screen flashed the word *educator*.

"Educator means sharing research-based information with people that they can choose to use or not use." Ruskie stopped and looked around the room to see who was alert and taking notes. He had his "special Extension agents," those who sucked up to him. They did this by always agreeing with him and taking pages of notes at meetings such as this.

"And that's where it stops. We share information with whoever wants it, and we try to do it effectively and efficiently. Computers can help us do that."

"What we don't do—and I want to underline this—we don't get in the middle of a squabble between an organic farmer and a big commercial farmer or when some crazy environmentalist might be going after a farmer whose manure might be trickling into a stream. We stay away from those battles. We end up getting bruised and get a bunch of bad publicity. And with the budget situation the way it is these days, we don't need any more bad publicity."

I looked at Sarah when he said this, and she rolled her eyes. We'd often talked about Ben Ruskie, his leadership style, and mostly about his short-sighted definition of what an educator should be doing.

"And something else I need to say to all of you as we look ahead, something very important." With the word *important* still hanging in the air, the courthouse's fire alarm went off. A high-pitched, piercing screech continued as we all hurried to the exits and stood outside on the courthouse lawn. In a couple of minutes, we heard fire trucks screaming toward the courthouse.

"Wonder what that last very important thing was?" I whispered to Sarah. She smiled.

20
Petition

Sarah and I never found out what that last important thing was. We decided not to wait and find out if the fire alarm was for real and the place was on fire or if someone had set it off as a prank. We hopped in the pickup and drove back to Willow River. I wondered if maybe one of the anti-government people had set off the alarm just to be mean and maybe to remind us once more that we really weren't wanted or needed anymore. I had smelled no smoke, and I heard no one yelling fire.

I remembered when these district meetings were interesting and useful, but they tend to have one major theme these days. Our budgets are being cut, and we'd better learn to do more than less. And the Internet is the way to do it. The Internet may help, but for me and my old-fashioned ideas, nothing beats sitting down with a person face-to-face, listening to their problems, hearing the questions, and working with that person to figure out a solution. Problem solving we called it. Facts from the Internet may help, but there is so much more to being a good teacher than merely providing facts, providing information. These days, many people are completely overloaded with information, some of it misinformation. They desperately need someone to help them sort out which information is based on facts, which is opinion without backup evidence, and which is an outright lie. Once sorted out, as educators, we help people decide which information fits their situation and which does not. Part of problem solving usually involves helping people figure out the economics of the information—can they afford to do what the information suggests? Or, in some instances, can they afford not to accept new information if they want to continue doing what they are doing now—continue to make a living on the land? This is the circumstance of many people I work with in Ames County.

Sarah sat quietly beside me as we drove north from Portage on the interstate, past Endeavor, Westfield, and Coloma. Past huge fields of potatoes with irrigation sweeps moving slowly across, providing the ever-thirsty crop with water. Past fields of peas, soon ready for harvesting, and fields of snap beans and sweet corn. All up and growing. Looking good.

But I was thinking about my meeting with the property owners on Winter Lake. They surely have a point, with considerable research backing them up, that too much irrigation is drawing down the level of their lake. I thought, *What can I do about it?* It's become a nasty political issue. The Eagle Party, with considerable clout in the legislature, wants to get rid of all regulations. Their motto: "Get the government out of the lives of people," surely doesn't help. I've long believed, and I think I'm right, that one role of the government is to make sure that one group of people doesn't have an unfair advantage over another group. Regulations are there to keep things in balance.

And, of course, not to forget the environmental people who see regulations concerning water, land, and air as necessary to ensure that future generations will have a decent place to live.

I hate getting involved in these political squabbles, and I know that Ben Ruskie would be on my case more than he already has as he's heard about my attempts to bring opposing groups together, to get them talking to each other, and maybe, just maybe as they get to know each other that they could work out some compromises that will allow these opposing groups to exist together in some kind of working harmony. I think this is one of my high-priority jobs as an educator.

The university has long had a reputation for not taking sides but trying to provide educational opportunities to all of Wisconsin's citizens. I see myself as a neutral broker when I try to bring opposing groups together. Of course, some groups, especially a large segment of the Eagle Party, see us as the problem—another government agency messing in the lives of people. "Let people work it out for themselves," they proclaim. "We don't need you high-paid government people trying to make things better." But I believe strongly that when people can't work through their problems and challenges by themselves, they sometimes need an outsider, someone with a broader perspective, to help them.

Of course, that's not to discount people's problem-solving abilities, especially those of rural people. Many of them have seen years of tough times, poor milk and livestock prices, corn and soybean prices like a roller coaster, one year high and the next year in the tank. Drought for the farmers who do not have irrigation, and that's most of them. Disease that attacks their crops. A farm accident that incapacitates someone in the family who has been a major contributor to the work that needs doing. Rural people are survivors, no question about it. But sometimes just a little outside help, a new research finding, a new way of thinking about a problem, can make a tremendous difference. This is where the county agents come in and where they can make life just a little bit easier for the country person who has lived a life filled with problems and challenges.

Sarah was politely listening to my long sermon on an educator's role in today's society, occasionally shaking her head in agreement.

"Well, what do you think about all this, Sarah?" I asked.

"I think we should get married and move to some other place," she said, smiling.

Arriving back at the courthouse in Willow River, Sarah and I headed to our respective offices. There were always emails to answer and phone calls to return.

Gladys had left the latest copy of the *Ames County Gazette* on the corner of my desk. I picked it up and read the headlines that shouted:

"Ames County Eagle Party Offers Petition to Close Down Extension Office"

I began reading the front-page article:

The Eagle Party of Ames County voted unanimously to solicit signatures from the "hardworking taxpayers of Ames County" to close down the University Extension Office in Ames County. Mike Braun, Chair of Ames County's Eagle Party said, "The sooner we can decrease the number of government workers in this state and country, the better off we will all be. Let's start by removing the Ames County University Extension Office, which has outlived its usefulness, as far as I can see."

The Ames County University Extension Office has been in Ames County since 1914 and is Ames County's direct link to Badger State University in Madison. Their ongoing educational programs include 4-H clubs, an out-of-school practical learn-by-doing education program for young people, ongoing educational programming focusing on family living and consumer questions, including nutrition education and family money management, a far-reaching program for community economic development, plus many programs designed for farmers and farm families.

Mike Braun said, "Starting next week, we will begin collecting signatures of taxpayers throughout Ames County who agree with us, and I know there are many who do. We must work hard to get the government off the backs of our citizens."

21
Mike Braun

I read the news article once more. *This Eagle Party is something else,* I thought. *What will they do next?* I was growing more convinced that Braun had thrown the rock through the window during our meeting and sent me the threatening letters. I also wondered what I should do about the article in the paper and the petition. Lots of people will probably sign it, and in doing so, they won't realize that when they sign their names, they are asking for the elimination of the Ames County 4-H program and the special nutrition programs that have been extremely popular. By signing, they are advocating doing away with the master gardener program that has helped gardeners small and large. And their signature would likely end the Ames County Fair, which has been an Ames County institution for more than a hundred years. And most of all, by signing the petition they are advocating cutting the county's direct tie to Badger State University and all of its resources that can and have flowed through the Ames County University Extension Office.

As I thought about all of this, I could feel a massive headache coming on—the kind of headache I occasionally got when I didn't know where to turn or what to do next.

I picked up the newspaper and headed toward Sarah's office. She was on the phone, so I sat down in a chair after she motioned me to do so. We tried to maintain a professional relationship in the office, but we both smiled inwardly because we knew our relationship with each other went well beyond what a professional relationship entailed.

Sarah hung up her phone. I dropped the newspaper on her desk. I watched as she read the headline and then the story. When Sarah was upset about something, a deep furrow developed on her forehead. I'm sure she wasn't even aware that it was there, but as I've come to know her so well, I have seen it several times over the years.

"Well," I said when she looked up.

"This the same Mike Braun that you tangled with at Winter Lake?"

"One and the same," I said. "He's out to get us, that's for darn sure."

"Who is this guy anyway, and what's he got stuck in his craw? Does he run one of the small businesses in the county?"

"Nope. He's a retired business manager from Chicago who bought a house on Winter Lake and, with his wife, moved out there when the lake level was still high. He's mad as hell that the water level of Winter Lake has dropped by about half—and still dropping. And he blames me for it all."

"Blames you, why?"

"Well, he says as a government worker, I am the one who taught big farmers around Winter Lake how to irrigate their crops and thus how to dry up his lake."

"Geez, that's a stretch," Sarah said.

"Well, he's somewhat got a point. I do work with the vegetable growers, and I did provide them with the recent research about the water needs of various vegetables, as well as research on irrigation practices that used a minimum amount of water for maximum effect." I continued, "There is good research and evidence that too many deep irrigation wells can have a negative effect on the aquifer, and especially lakes like Winter Lake that rise and fall with groundwater levels. But what Braun fails to understand is that our office doesn't grant the permits for these deep-well irrigation units. He should take his argument to the Department of Natural Resources. They are the ones who grant the permits for the wells. They've probably granted too many, but that's not for me to say."

"Did you tell Braun about the permitting situation and that we have nothing to do with it?"

"Unfortunately, Braun left the meeting in a huff before I had a chance to explain any of this. But even if he knew the Department of Natural Resources' role, his position would likely be to eliminate the DNR. He'd probably say they were just another bunch of overpaid government workers making life difficult for everyone."

"This kind of news story surely doesn't help us, Scott. Especially after hearing from Ben Ruskie that we're likely to see more budget cuts in the future. Our state legislature listens to these people."

"So, what should we do? Write a rebuttal to the story, saying how much we do and how important it is to the people of Ames County?" I offered. I picked up the article and read it once more.

"I wouldn't do that. I remember my dad saying something along the lines that if you get stung by a hornet, you don't want to take a stick and wrack the hornet's nest. What will happen is you'll get stung even worse," Sarah said.

"You're probably right. I was thinking I might go out to Winter Lake and have a talk with Braun—one-to-one."

"You think he'll talk with you? From what you've said, I don't think so. We've got to think of another way to get to him and thus to his band of no-government followers—maybe a larger group of people than we think. But I think way over half the people in this county support what we're doing and would really be upset if we were forced to close up shop," said Sarah.

"We've got to think of something, Sarah. I'm sure that Greg at the paper might have some ideas. We should talk with him. I know he's got to stay neutral in all of this if he wants to keep his subscribers, but I also know he very much supports what we're doing. After our planning council meeting tomorrow, let's ask him to stay on for a bit, and we'll have a chat with him."

"That sounds like a reasonable start," said Sarah. Then she looked right at me with that furrow in her forehead, deeper than usual. "We can't ignore this, Scott. Braun and his anti-government group could surely destroy what we're trying to do with the planning council. And if they get a bunch of signatures on their petition, our office may be closing."

"In my ten years here I've never seen anything like this. Ames County is coming apart at the seams. And we're right in the middle of it. What time is it?"

Sarah glanced at her watch. "It's five-thirty."

"I've got a splitting headache. I'm going home," I said.

"Come over to my place for supper, and we'll work on that headache." Sarah smiled.

On the same page of the *Gazette* that carried the upsetting Eagle Party article was the first retired farmer article:

"Remembering Lamps and Lanterns"
By Oscar Anderson

Back during World War II, in the early 1940s, we farmed without electricity. All of our neighbors did. Today, it's hard to believe that we could survive doing it, but we did. In the house we used kerosene lamps—we had one in the kitchen, a second one in the dining room, and a third, smaller one I that used to find my way to my bedroom during the long, dark nights of winter.

For the outside chores, we used barn lanterns, the kind with a globe that was protected with a heavy steel wire and which had a carrying handle that could also be used to hang it on a nail in the barn, in the granary, the pump house, wherever we were working.

In those days, Pa and I milked cows by hand. I'd hang my lantern on a nail on the end of the barn, and Pa would hang his lantern on a nail on the other end. That was all the light we had, but it was enough to get the job done. We could see well enough to milk the cows, as well as feed them grain, silage, and hay.

Would you believe that in those days, kerosene was only fifteen cents a gallon, and a gallon would last us about a week? Pretty cheap light, I must say, especially when I compare it to the electric bills I pay today.

One of the most interesting things I remember about the barn lantern was carrying it up into the barn's haymow on a below-

zero day. It was warm and cozy in the lower part of the barn, where the cattle and our team of horses were housed, but the haymow was nearly as cold as it was outside. Some of the warm air created by the livestock made its way to the haymow above them, and this warm air, when it struck the enormous cobwebs everywhere, turned to frost. I'm not much for saying good things about cobwebs, but these frost-covered cobwebs were absolutely beautiful.

I remember well when we finally got electricity on our farm. In the summer of 1946, Pa had hired a couple of electricians to wire the farm, which meant stringing wires to the barn, the pump house, the granary, the chicken house, the machine shed, and our farmhouse. It took them more than two weeks. I remember one of the electricians asking Pa if they should string wires to the outhouse that stood a short distance from the north side of the house. Pa told them not to. He said "What goes on in that little building don't need no electric light."

It wasn't until April 1947 that electricity finally arrived at the farm. I was attending country school at the time, and when I arrived home on that rather cloudy and dreary April afternoon, Pa said, "We're hooked up." His words meant that the newly erected electric pole that stood near our mailbox alongside the road now had the electric transformer in place and that electricity flowed from it to our buildings.

It took some adjusting for all of us, because now, with but the flip of a switch, we could have brilliant light nearly everywhere. I remember my mother spending the better part of two weeks cleaning because she could now see dust that had been hidden in shadows when we lighted the house with kerosene lamps.

I also remember the first time when we flipped on the lights behind our cows, and rather than two barn lanterns creating a dim yellow light with lots of shadows, the entire barn was ablaze with white light. The cows didn't know what was going on and began fidgeting, looking around, and making a mess, which is what cows do when they are excited. It took the cows more than a week to adjust to this new environment.

When the lights came on in the barn, the cats ran for cover, unsure of what to make of this new thing that had made everything bright and eliminated the shadows where the cats often found the mice that it was their job to catch.

Those are some of the things I remember about lamps and lanterns and the day that electricity came to our farm and changed everything. It made life easier, that's for sure. But it also made life more complicated, as we soon bought an electric-powered milking machine, added more cows, and considered building a new barn as our herd grew larger.

22
To-Do List

With all the fuss and fury that had been going on, I looked forward to our next meeting of the planning council. I was wondering how Jodi Henderson would run the meeting. I had expected that she might call and talk about how she might do it. But she didn't. The meeting was set for one o'clock in the afternoon, and at quarter to one, people began arriving, including Jodi Henderson representing the Small-Acreage Farmers Association; Harvey Rivers from the Ames County Historical Society; John Flyer from the John Deere dealership; Jeff Miles representing the Willow River Bank; Bill Workman, president of the Ames County Farm Bureau; Emil Barnes, president of the Ames County Farmers Union; Jill Varsac, representing CFTF; and Greg Charter, editor of the *Ames County Gazette*. And then, a minute before one, George Emerson, representing the Winter Lake property owners, arrived.

I thanked George for coming, introduced him to the group and said he would be joining them. Then I turned the meeting over to Jodi and sat down.

"Okay, before we get down to the serious matters of this meeting, I believe we should spend a few minutes becoming centered and relaxed," said Jodi.

Looking around the room, I could see several strange looks.

"You've all heard of yoga, right?"

Several people's hands went all the way up—some only halfway, as if they weren't sure they wanted to admit they knew.

"Well, I'm going to introduce you to a simple yoga exercise before we get started with the meeting. I've been doing yoga exercises for several years, and it has helped me. Helped me a lot. As many of you know, yoga is an ancient art that attempts to bring together the body, mind, and spirit. The simple exercise I have today is good for the back. So, it's practical, too."

With that little talk about the virtues of yoga, I wondered how many of our group would actually do one of the exercises. I soon would find out.

"Okay, everybody. Up and out of your chairs," Jodi instructed.

To my surprise, everyone stood up. The inflection in Jodi's voice left no alternative. Nothing tentative in her voice. The expectation— everyone would participate.

"Now, here is what I want you to do. I'll demonstrate first," she said as she walked to the front of the room, where there was a little extra space. She placed her right foot firmly on the floor, then extended her left leg behind her as far as it would go, all the while bending forward so that her right hand touched the floor by her right foot. She held her left arm high in the air. "I want you all to do this, and as you do, breathe deeply." She illustrated this by taking several deep breaths.

"Any questions?"

"What if I can't bend over that far," Bill asked. I was surprised that he was even thinking of doing the exercise.

"Bend as far as you can," said Jodi, smiling.

"Okay, let's do it." To my great surprise, everyone did it or tried to. Amazing. I would never have tried doing something like this, but I did it, too. Had to. It was my idea to turn our meetings over to different members of the group. It's the risk you take when you do this. You gotta go with what the temporary leader suggests. If she suggests doing yoga, well you do yoga. I wondered what the members of the county board would think if they saw us doing yoga exercises in the University Extension Office. And what would the anti-government folks do if they knew what went on in the Extension Office? Guys like Mike Braun would have a field day. But all these thoughts disappeared when Jodi said, "Okay, back in your chairs. Feeling better? Feeling relaxed?"

"I think I pulled a muscle," said Greg. He said it with a big smile on his face. Everyone laughed. I laughed. Who would have thought that doing something as simple as a yoga exercise might bring a potentially quite divisive group together? Not me, for sure. It may have been a stroke of genius on my part to ask Jodi to chair the meeting—maybe not. We'll see how all of this goes.

"Scott has prepared a list of the ideas we brainstormed the first time we met," Jodi continued. She gave each person a copy of the list.

"Our task, if I could try and summarize what we talked about at our first meeting, is to do something to bring our agricultural community together as well as help the general public learn a bit more about where their food comes from. Does anyone see our purpose any differently?"

George Emerson raised his hand. "I'm new to this group, but I'm wondering if this planning council will get around to discussing such practical matters as to why some of the lakes in western Ames County are drying up. My neighbors on Winter Lake and I believe it's the fault of the big-acreage vegetable farmers and their massive irrigation systems."

"I would think that might be a reasonable topic for us to discuss," Jodi said as she looked toward me for approval. I smiled but didn't say anything. I wanted this group to own its agenda. I'll help, but the group's got to decide on its purpose and how it wants to accomplish it.

A moment of silence.

"What George suggests reminds me that maybe we've put the cart before the horse with our list of activities," Jodi said, pausing before she went on. "Maybe we should put the reasons for carrying out these various activities right out in front of us, so we know what problems, what concerns, we're trying to deal with by working through the items on this list."

She looked around the room to see the reaction to her thought. I had considered doing this at the first meeting but decided not to because I didn't want this planning council to get into a big harangue about what was a problem and what was not—so I chickened out and decided to go with solutions to problems that I assumed everyone knew about. Jodi is right. We should start with the problem before working on a solution.

Jodi walked up to the whiteboard. She wrote in big block letters across the top of the board "AMES COUNTY AG CHALLENGES AND ISSUES." Then she wrote "Irrigation and declining lake levels."

"Well," said Greg, "from my perspective running the *Ames County Gazette*, I believe these are some of the issues we might deal with and that I hear about nearly every day." He paused for a minute. "Now I just want to put these out there, not for us to debate today as to which one is more important than another, but just to get them out there." He paused again and looked at reactions from people sitting around the table.

I knew Greg well enough that he had an uncanny ability to read people's reactions from their body language, their facial expressions, what they did with their hands, and how they sat in their chairs.

"Well, here goes," he said. "Disagreement between industrial-size farmers and small-acreage farmers."

Jodi quickly wrote these words on the whiteboard.

"Unpredictable prices for farm products," Greg said. "Whenever I talk with a farmer, the discussion always gets around to that issue."

Jodi wrote the topic on the whiteboard.

"I've got a couple more, but I think I'll give other people a chance to share," said Greg.

"Alright. What are some more issues facing Ames County agriculture?" asked Jodi as she looked around the table.

"Well," began Emil, who represented the Farmers Union members in the group. "We're losing family farms left and right. These family farms—and there were once thousands of them—made this country what it is today. Provided the values that were and are so important for a democracy."

Jodi wrote "Loss of family farms" on the whiteboard.

Bill held up his hand. "Scott is very quiet about this, but I think it should be shared with everyone around this table. Some of you were at the meeting when a rock was thrown through a window and disrupted a meeting that Scott had called. Wrapped around that rock was a threatening letter demanding that Scott leave his position here in Ames County. And not long after that, he got another letter threatening the same. These letters threatened harm to Scott unless he leaves Ames County."

There were several looks of astonishment as Bill shared this information.

"Who is behind something like that? You show the letters to the police?" asked Jodi.

"Yes, the police are looking into it—it's no big deal," I said, trying not to show how upset I was about it. "We don't know who did it. Police aren't too sure we'll ever find out, either."

"Well," said Bill, "I believe somebody in that Eagle Party anti-government group is behind it. That's who I think did it."

I was surprised that George didn't mention Mike Braun and how he went off on me when I met with the Winter Lake owners.

Bill continued, "You probably all saw the article in the *Gazette* about how the Eagle Party's anti-government group is trying to get people in the county to close down this office. The article mentioned Mike Braun as heading up that group."

"That's correct," said Greg.

Jodi wrote in large letters "GROUP WANTS TO CLOSE EXT. OFFICE."

"Wow," said Jodi as she stood back and eyed the list. "Dare I ask if there are any more issues?"

"Yes, I'd like to add one," said John, the John Deere dealer. Flyer had said nothing at the meeting so far.

"I'd like to add this issue. It's a bit broad and difficult to deal with." He stopped for a minute. "I think we should add to the list that a growing number of people don't know where their food comes from and how important farmers are so that we all have something to eat, no matter what kind of a farmer they are."

Jodi wrote: "Public doesn't know the importance of farmers." Then she looked at Flyer and asked, "Does that cover it, Mr. Flyer?"

"Pretty much. And please call me John."

"Jeff, you haven't had a chance to say anything. Do you have an issue to add to this list?"

"I don't. What I see in front of us looks pretty good to me."

Jill Varsac quietly said, "Sometimes I wonder why I am a part of this group."

So far, she had said nothing, but everyone around the table knew of her group's strong feelings about the environment and her often strident writings about how big agriculture was ruining the environment.

"Water," said Jill.

"Water?" Jodi said, looking at Jill for an explanation.

"Yes, water. Clean, abundant, readily available water. It's one of the biggest issues this country and the world faces."

Jodi wrote "Water" on the whiteboard. I looked around the room to see reactions from the group. All I saw was a slight grin on George Emerson's face.

"Is that it for the moment?" Jodi asked, looking around the table.

"One more I'd like to add," said Jill Varsac. She hesitated for a moment before going on because she knew how contentious this issue had become and how it had divided not only Ames County, the state of Wisconsin but the entire country.

"Climate change," Jill said. "Without paying attention to climate change, farming as we know it today will have no future."

Jodi wrote "Climate change" on the board. Everyone was now staring at the whiteboard and the words written there. No one said a word.

"Well, I think we should add, 'Rural history not well known,'" said Harvey, breaking the silence. Jodi added the item to the list.

The group sat back and looked at what Jodi had written on the whiteboard:

Ames County Agricultural Issues and Challenges

1. Irrigation and declining lake levels
2. Disagreement between industrial-size farmers and small-acreage farmers
3. Unpredictable markets and prices for farm products
4. Loss of family farms
5. Group wants to close Ext. office
6. Public doesn't know the importance of farmers
7. Water
8. Climate change
9. Rural history not well known

"I suggest we take a fifteen-minute break and come back and figure out what we do next."

23

Mike Braun Loses It

When I returned to the outer office, Gladys said, "You'd better return this phone call." She handed me a slip of paper with the name Mike Braun and a phone number written on it. I'd never seen Gladys with a more serious look on her face. I went into my office, closed the door, and punched in the numbers.

"This is Mike Braun," a voice said. It was angry, more like a growl.

"Scott Olson here," I said, trying to use my most professional voice.

"You remember me, doncha?" Braun asked.

"Yes, I remember you."

"Well, you know about the petition my people are sending around, the one asking people to sign saying your damn office oughta be closed."

"Yes, I know about the petition," I said, trying to keep the deep anger I felt out of my voice.

"Well, I just wanted you to know that your sneaky efforts to keep the good, law-abiding, taxpaying citizens living here in Ames County from signing the petition are gonna backfire on you."

"What are you talking about?"

"You damn well know what I'm talking about. This here women's group that your office sponsors. Let's see, they call themselves the Ames County Homemakers. Well you know what they did?"

I was afraid to ask, but I did. "What did they do?"

"You damn well know what they did, you and that frizzy woman that works in your office, what's her name—Sarah somebody. In their last Homemakers newsletter there was a note from the president of the group. Some old broad whose name I don't remember wrote that nobody should sign our petition."

"Oh," was all I could think to say.

"Well, I've hired an attorney, and I'm gonna sue your ass for trying to interfere with democracy. You can't tell people they shouldn't sign a petition. It's against the law. You ought to know that, bein' a government worker and all."

I wanted to say to Mike Braun that I didn't tell anybody that they shouldn't sign his petition, and I also wanted to tell him that the Homemakers Organization has every right to do what it did. In fact, I was quite pleased to hear about it. But I didn't want to dignify Mike with a response.

"Thanks for giving me this information," I said and hung up. I suspect doing so infuriated Mike even more. But I must say I felt good about doing it.

I sat back in my chair and rubbed my eyes. I could feel a huge headache coming on. *Besides all that I have on my plate, now I've got to deal with a lawsuit. What next?*

There was a quiet knock on the door.

"The group is back from their break and is waiting for you, Scott."

"Tell them I'll be right there." I pulled open the bottom drawer in my desk, took out a couple of aspirins, and walked down the hall to the washroom, where I drank some water and downed the aspirins. I returned to the meeting room, hoping my face didn't show the anger I felt.

"Okay," said Jodi, once more taking charge of the meeting.

I must say I was impressed with this young woman. I didn't know that she had these leadership skills. I was happy I asked her to chair this meeting, but now I wondered what she would do next. Some issues on the board, especially "Climate change," were like dumping kerosene on a smoldering fire. I looked forward to how she would handle this.

"Let's take a look at the list of issues we believe Ames County agriculture is facing," she said. "Is there anything on the list that shouldn't be there?"

1. Irrigation and declining lake levels
2. Disagreement between industrial-size farmers and small-acreage farmers
3. Unpredictable markets and prices for farm products
4. Loss of family farms
5. Group wants to close Ext. office
6. Public doesn't know the importance of farmers
7. Water
8. Climate change
9. Rural history not well known

The room was quiet as everyone looked over the list of nine items.

After a brief pause, Bill said, "I'm not so sure that we should leave "Climate change" on our list. I know a bunch of people who believe it's just a hoax."

Once more there was silence, indicating no support for removing it from the list.

"Anything else that should be added or removed from the list?" Jodi asked. I held up my hand. "I think we should cross off 'Saving our Extension Office,'" I said. "I don't want to sound ungrateful, but I don't think we should focus on that as one of our major activities. And again, don't misunderstand me, but I don't want the public to see this planning council as some kind of rubber stamp for the Extension Office. Besides, what this planning council does and how it does it will surely reflect well on this office."

I no more than got the words out of my mouth when we heard a loud voice in the outer office.

"Excuse me a minute," I said. I opened the door and saw Mike Braun, red-faced and standing in front of the desk where a frightened Gladys sat, her face white as a sheet. I quickly could see why. Mike Braun was wearing a pistol on his belt, and he rested one hand on the butt of the weapon.

"There you are," yelled Braun, the veins in his neck throbbing. "You hung up on me a while ago. You're a coward. That's what you are—a damn coward. I wasn't through talkin' to you. I was here in town, doin' some business when I called. So here I am in person. I'm gonna finish what I had to say, and you'd damn well better listen this time," he yelled. I was hoping that Gladys would have a chance to call 911. Out of the corner of my eye, I saw her reach for the phone.

"Woman, put down that damn phone. I'm here to talk with this jackass of a government worker, and this time he's gonna hear me out." Once more, he put his right hand on the butt of his pistol.

"Okay," I said, holding up both hands. "Calm down. I'll listen. Come into my office, where we can both sit and be a bit more comfortable."

"I'm not goin' into your damn office and give this woman a chance to call 911. What I've got to say, I'm gonna say right here. While we're both standin' up and facin' each other." He touched his right hand to the butt of his pistol again.

Out of the corner of my eye I noticed that the door to the conference room had slowly opened, and George and Greg quietly moved behind Braun.

"You keep tryin' to interfere with our petition to close this office. Well, you'll—"

He didn't get to finish the sentence. Emerson grabbed him by one arm and Charter by the other. He struggled for a bit. But then, when he noticed that one of those holding his arm was his neighbor, he quit struggling.

"George, what in hell are you doin' here? In this damn government office. You sold out to the damn government, too?"

Gladys picked up the phone.

"Don't have to call 911," George said. "We'll take care of it. Mike Braun's my neighbor out on Winter Lake."

"Get your damn hands off me," said Braun. "I didn't mean this miserable excuse for a person no harm. Just wanted to get his attention a little. Pistol isn't even loaded."

"Mike, you've been drinking. You'd better go home," said George.

"And the next time you come to town, I'd suggest you leave your gun at home. Carrying that gun is only going to get you into trouble."

"Man's gotta protect himself. Can't trust the police to do it anymore. They're part of the damn government, too. Gotta protect ourselves," said Mike, his speech somewhat slurred.

George took hold of Braun's arm and steered him toward the door.

"I'll help Mike to his car and drive him home," George said to me.

With Mike out the door, the planning council members looked at each other in disbelief. "Well, that was something," said Jodi. She turned to me. "What do we do?"

"Who can meet a week from today?" I asked. "That will give you all a chance to mull over the decisions we made today so we can move on to deciding what kind of activities we might plan. Besides, after all of this, it will be a little hard to concentrate if we keep going today."

Heads shook in agreement, and, unbelievably, everyone said they could make the next meeting. The last one to leave was Jeff Miles. I heard him ask, "Is Sarah in?" "Thought I would say hello if she was."

"No, Sarah's at a meeting out of town today," Gladys said. "I'll tell her you asked." The exchange between Gladys and Jeff seemed innocuous enough, and yet was there more to it? *Is there something going on with Jeff that I don't know?* I thought.

"Thanks," Jeff said as he left.

"Sounds like Jeff still has a thing for Sarah," said Gladys.

"Does, doesn't it?"

24
What Next?

After everyone left, the office was mostly quiet, save for the occasional phone call that Gladys was taking and answering without bothering me. I can never thank Gladys enough for handling the majority of the phone calls herself. The questions that come in, one after the other, day after day: "What variety of strawberries should I plant?" "When should I set out tomato plants?" "I think there's a raccoon under my porch. What do I do?" Gladys had the answer to these questions. Most of them she had heard before.

I heard Sarah return and talk briefly with Gladys before returning to her office. I decided I'd best share with Sarah what had happened earlier this afternoon. I don't know what I would do without having her to lean on when problems began piling up deeper than I could handle.

I knocked on her door. "Come in," she said. She was working at her computer, no doubt working through the long list of emails each of us received daily. When she saw that it was me, she smiled. "So, how's your day been going?"

"As a matter of fact, not so good," I said, trying to keep my voice steady and without emotion. But Sarah knew me too well to know something serious must have happened.

"Well, the planning council met here right after lunch, and we were making good progress. We were just about ready to discuss putting some plans into action when I heard yelling in the outer office."

I then went on to explain how gun-toting Mike Braun from Winter Lake was yelling at Gladys and then proceeded to yell at me, all the while with his hand on the butt of his pistol. "To tell you the truth, I was scared out of my wits. Never had a gun-toting person yell at me. Looked like any minute he'd pull out his gun and start shooting."

"Wow!" was all Sarah said. "Wow. You call the police?"

"Gladys tried to, but he wouldn't let her. That Mike Braun is a nutcase."

"So, what happened?" I explained how Braun's neighbor George Emerson, the lawyer, and Greg Charter from the paper snuck up behind him, grabbed his arms, and probably prevented a catastrophe.

"Then did you call the police?"

"We didn't. Emerson said he'd take care of Braun. He had been drinking, and I think that Emerson saved his hide. I suspect I could have pressed charges."

"Well, my God, Scott. This wild man could have shot you. Killed you right here in the office."

"I don't know. He's mostly mad as hell that the county's Homemakers Organization has asked its members not to sign this petition that his anti-government group is passing around the county. He said I told these women not to sign the petition. By the way, did you say anything to the group about it?"

"I take the Fifth Amendment," said Sarah, smiling broadly. "So, are you gonna report this to Chief Wilkins?"

"I don't think so. If I do, all it will accomplish is adding a little more kerosene to the fire, which already has flames shooting high into the air."

"Scott, you've got to tell Chief Wilkins about this. You really do. You don't have to press charges, but he needs to know about this, especially after the couple of threatening letters you've gotten and the go-around you had with Braun when you were at the meeting at Winter Lake."

"Wouldn't hurt to tell him, I suppose," I said. "But I don't want him going after Braun unless he does something really stupid. Like shooting somebody."

"Scott, that somebody could be you. It could be you." Sarah looked right at me with that serious look she sometimes gets.

"Okay, okay. I'll let Wilkins know." I got up to leave. "Oh, by the way, Jeff Miles asked about you. He seemed disappointed when Gladys told him you were away at a meeting," I said this with a bit of a smirk because I knew how Sarah felt about this old boyfriend and how she did not want to be bothered by him or so much as want to talk with him.

"That guy never gives up, does he?" Sarah said. Frowning, she turned back to her computer screen.

Once back in my office, I found the private number that Chief Wilkins had given me after I'd shared the threatening letters with him. I punched in the numbers.

"Chief Wilkins," I heard after the second ring.

"This is Scott Olson over at the Extension Office," I said.

"How you doin,' Scott?" Wilkins said.

"As a matter of fact, not so good."

"So, what's going on? Another threatening letter?"

"Worse. Do you know Mike Braun, who lives out at Winter Lake?"

"Yeah, I've heard of this guy. Read about him in the paper the other day. He's head of this anti-government bunch in the Eagle Party. What about him?"

"Well, he stopped in the office earlier this afternoon, yelling his fool head off about how I asked people not to sign his petition to close down the Extension Office. He'd obviously been drinking. He disrupted a meeting we were holding, and besides that, he was wearing a pistol on his belt. As he yelled, he kept putting his hand on the butt of the gun."

"So, you want me to arrest the guy?"

"No, no, I don't want to press charges. Not yet, anyway. He really didn't hurt anyone. But I must say he scared the bejeebers out of everybody on the council besides poor Gladys, who had to deal with him first."

"What do you want me to do?"

"Right now, nothing. But if the crime lab and your detective can figure out a way of tracing those letters to Braun, then that will change things."

"Scott, a word of advice. You are walking on eggshells; you know that, don't you? You want a permit to carry? I'll help you get one, and I'll even lend you one of my personal guns. I've got a 9mm Beretta in my desk drawer that you are welcome to use."

"Thanks, Chief, but I don't think so. I'm a lousy shot. I'd probably end up shooting myself in the foot."

"Think about it, Scott. And you watch out for yourself."

I hung up the phone and sat back in my chair. Whoever heard of a county agricultural agent running around with a gun in his pocket? I sure hope it hasn't come to that.

25
Farm Memories

Ames County Gazette

As we explained in a previous issue, the Gazette will be running a series of stories written by farmers describing farm life as they remembered it from an earlier day. In this issue, we have included a story written by octogenarian Fred Russo, who has farmed in Ames County all of his life, as his father before him did.

The Gazette also plans to run stories written by retired farm women, recalling the role of women on the farm fifty-plus years ago. Send the stories to: Editor, Ames County Gazette, Willow River, Wisconsin.

This issue's story features memories of threshing days on the farm.

"Memories of Threshing"
By Fred Russo, Link Lake

I'm eighty-four years old, and I remember threshing grain when I was a kid. There were no combines to cut the grain and thresh it at the same time. Each of us farmers in those days cut our grain with a grain binder pulled by a team of horses. Every farmer in our neighborhood grew about twenty acres of oats; a few maybe had thirty acres. Once the oats were cut, we'd stand the oat bundles in shocks that spread out from one end of the oat field to the other. It was a sight to see, all them oat shocks standing like so many soldiers at attention.

After the oat shocks had stood for a week or so, long enough so the oats would be good and dry, a threshing machine came into the neighborhood. What a sight it was to see that big dusty threshing machine pulled by a John Deere R tractor drive into our farmyard. It was one of the first diesel tractors I ever saw.

Pa invited all the neighbors to help out. Some hauled oat bundles with their teams and wagons from the oat field. Some helped carry sacks of threshed grain from the threshing machine to the granary. One older neighbor was in charge of building the straw stack. He steered the big blower pipe back and forth as the yellow oat straw spewed out of its end.

At noon, we had the biggest meal you could ever imagine. Meat and potatoes and fresh vegetables. All the coffee you could drink and two or three different kinds of pie—apple, cherry, sometimes strawberry. After the big meal the whole crew would gather under our big shade tree by the kitchen porch and rest and tell stories. What wonderful stories they were—stories about the Depression and the hobos that would stop by our farms for something to eat. Stories about fishing and hunting. About rainstorms and strong winds. It was a way for us to get to know our neighbors as well as we knew the members of our own family. We all worked together in those days. We had to. We depended on our neighbors, and they depended on us. It didn't matter what our nationality or religion or our politics.

When our grain was threshed, we'd all move to the next farm and do it all over again, and to the next and the next until everyone's grain was threshed. It's one of the best memories of my early farm life.

Oscar Anderson arrived at the Black Oak Café a few minutes before his friend Fred Russo. Both retired farmers met weekly to visit over coffee. Oscar was halfway through his first cup when Fred arrived, a little out of breath.

Fred anticipated some complaint from Oscar, who expected everyone to be on time, whether for a wedding, a funeral, or for a cup of coffee together.

Fred pulled off his John Deere cap and sat down opposite his old friend and neighbor, expecting a comment about him being five minutes late. But he heard something different.

"You popped off your buttons yet, Fred?" asked Oscar.

"Did I pop off what?" replied Fred.

"Your buttons."

"What in God's creation are you talking about? This here jacket's got a zipper. No buttons."

"You see this week's edition of the *Ames County Gazette*?"

"Nope, haven't seen it yet. What's that got to do with buttons?" asked Fred.

"It's got your story about threshing in it. And a darn good story it is."

"Well, thank you, Oscar. Your piece on lamps and lanterns wasn't too shabby either." They both raised their coffee cups with a salute to each other.

"Now let's hope somebody reads those stories," said Oscar. "You made a good point about when neighbors got along and helped each other. Maybe some of the folks that are squabbling with each other will learn something."

"Let's hope," said Fred as he took another sip of coffee.

26
Action Plans

Before the next planning council meeting, I decided I should do a little checking with some of the council members, especially the major agriculture leaders such as Emil Barnes, president of the Farmers Union, and Bill Workman, president of the Farm Bureau. I wanted to make sure I had both of these men on board, or what I was trying to accomplish would fail as miserably as the first meeting that resulted in a smashed window. I had worked with Farmers Union and Farm Bureau members over the years, trying to be fair and not playing favorites with either group.

First, I drove out to Bill's farm. I stopped at the house, and his wife said he was doing something out in the heifer barn. The heifer barn had once been the Workmans' main barn before they expanded their operation and built a sizable free-stall dairy barn for their milking cows. The old barn, which Bill told me was built in 1900, now housed their heifers before they had their first calves and were moved into the free-stall barn with its attached milking parlor.

I pulled open the barn door and spotted Bill. He was doing the yoga exercise that Jodi had taught at the last meeting of the planning council. I couldn't have been more surprised.

"Good morning, Bill," I said, not sure if I should comment on his doing a yoga exercise in front of some twenty-five young Holstein heifers who mostly ignored what he was doing.

"I'm doin' great for an old guy," Bill said, smiling. "This yoga stuff has really helped my back. I do this exercise every morning."

"Glad to hear it." I'd been concerned that folks attending the planning meeting had been turned off when asked to do yoga and were reluctant to say anything.

"I stopped by to see what your thoughts are about the planning council so far—what we should do that we haven't done. What we may have done that we shouldn't have done."

"Scott, you worry too much," Bill said. "I think the planning council is a great idea. We got a bunch of concerns out there for everyone to see. I don't know how much our little group can do to solve these problems—but it's a darn good start. And you know what? I'm impressed that we all remained civil toward each other. I really am. Folks sitting around that table represent a bunch of opposing positions. Take Jill Varsac for instance. Some of us farmers think all she and her environmental group want to do is close down agriculture. Well, that's not who she is. She was listening to the discussion."

"One of my major concerns these days is having the various agriculture and environmental people talking to each other, and not yelling when they do it. Too much yelling going on," I said.

"You got that right, Scott. I think the planning council is a good start toward at least people getting to know each other, even though they may not agree with each other."

"What should the planning council do next?" I asked.

Bill thought for a minute, rubbed his big, calloused hands together, and said, "I think we're ready to try one of the things we talked about at the first meeting—sponsor something that will get the different farmer groups and the urban folks together, rubbing shoulders with each other, getting to know each other a little better. Doing something together to get their minds off their differences."

"Exactly what I was thinking," I said. "I had that in mind back in April when somebody threw a rock through the window and broke up our meeting."

"By the way, Scott, has the police chief found out who did that and who sent you those threatening letters?"

"Nope, I haven't heard a word," I said, trying not to show that I was a lot more concerned about the letters than I was letting on.

"I've been thinking who might have done it. My guess is that guy who lives out on Winter Lake. That guy is scary. Running around drunk with a pistol strapped to his side. Police chief checking on him?"

"He is. Chief has sent the letters to the crime lab in Madison to see if they can find any fingerprints or anything else that might lead to the culprit," I said.

"Well, I hope they find him soon. He's a scary bugger. So is that Eagle Party and its anti-government tirade. Scary bunch."

I didn't want to mention that Bill's son, Paul, was a part of the group. He and Paul must have some interesting discussions about the Eagle Party's activities—or maybe they just didn't talk to each other about politics.

I thanked Bill and drove on to Emil's farm. He was working in his farm shop, doing some repairs on one of his tractors. I asked him the same questions I asked Bill, and, surprisingly, got almost the same answer. Emil was pleased with what the planning council was doing and was, like Bill, happy to see a group of people with divergent interests talking to each other in a civil way.

"Too much yelling going on these days," Emil said. "We get nowhere yelling at each other."

Emil also asked about the Eagle Party's petition to close down the Extension Office. I said I didn't know any more about how the petition was doing beyond what I read in the paper.

"That Eagle Party," Emil said, sighing. "What's this country coming to when we've got a bunch of ill-informed folks believing that getting rid of government workers will make their lives easier? I just don't understand it," Emil said. "Just don't understand it."

I didn't say anything, but I couldn't agree more with what Emil was saying. I changed the subject.

"What should the planning council be doing next?" I asked.

"I've been thinking about that," Emil said. "I think it's time we put on some kind of an event—let folks know that we not only talk about problems facing agriculture; we do something about it."

"You know what?" I said, smiling. "Bill Workman said the same thing."

"Bill's a good guy. Don't always agree with him, but every once in a while he'll come up with a good idea." Now Emil was smiling.

I drove back to the office feeling good. So far, the idea of the planning council seems to be working—at least we've got the council members talking with each other. Now, as both Bill and Emil suggested, it's time to plan an event that can be the start of bringing the larger Ames County community together. The ringer in the idea is the Eagle Party. I'm curious how many citizens in Ames County agree with their aggressive position on shutting down as much of the government as possible. They especially want to shut down the county Extension Office, which has been a prominent feature in Ames County since 1914. I'm also concerned that some of the people in this group seem prone to violence. I keep thinking about the rock thrown through the window of the community center back in early April when I was trying to get the farming groups to talk to each other. That surely didn't work. The follow-up threatening letter scared the crap out of me. I tried not to let my fear show, but it was impossible. In my entire life, I had never gotten anything close to a threatening letter.

And then Mike Braun. Wow, what a piece of work he was. There was no question about his intentions to close down our office. I wonder what he and his group of crazies will do next? Chief Wilkins warned me to watch my back. Sure made it difficult to sleep at night.

To add to my problems, all of us working for Badger State University Extension and located in Wisconsin counties will see another round of budget cuts.

"Expect about a 5 percent cut in our next annual budget," Ben Ruskie, my district supervisor, wrote. "We're likely faced with some more staff reductions." That's all he wrote—nothing about how his office was challenging the legislature's planned budget reductions, nothing about which programs might be cut and which staff fired. What a great way to keep up staff morale. The cynical side of me thought, *Mike Braun doesn't have to spend his time trying to shut down the Ames County Extension Office; the state legislature will do it for him.* Of course, the same Eagle Party wants to eliminate government programs and government workers at all levels, from the villages and cities to the counties and the state. And if they have their way, I suspect they'd work their way up to the federal government. I'm supposed to be nonpartisan and work with everyone, but it's hard to do that when one faction of my clientele wants to get me fired, no matter what I do and how hard I try to do it.

I've shared some of my thoughts with Sarah, and she is as concerned, maybe even more than I am. She's concerned that I'll be hurt one of these days, maybe even killed.

"Don't forget Mike Braun carried a gun into this office. Don't ever forget that." Sarah reminded me.

"Believe me, I haven't forgotten," I said. Then I told her that Chief Wilkins had confiscated Braun's gun. The chief told Braun that if he ever again showed up carrying a gun, he would toss him in jail.

"Braun's got friends, Scott," Sarah said. "I can image that some of them are just as crazy as he is."

I couldn't think of a good answer.

"All this budget cutting," Sarah said, moving away from concerns about Mike Braun. "Do the people of this great state of Wisconsin no longer believe what we're doing is worthwhile? Is that what's going on, Scott?"

"I can't believe that the majority of our citizens have closed the book on us. I just can't believe that. I think the Eagle Party is behind all this. They've got people believing that the state doesn't need much government, and with less government, their taxes will be lower. They've gotten a lot of people believing that taxes are bad and a waste of hardworking citizens' money," said Scott.

"Whatever happened to believing that taxes help all of us, especially those who don't have the resources to help themselves? And whatever happened to the idea that education at all levels helps to not only improve the people receiving it but helps to better the society as well?" asked Sarah.

I've always been impressed with Sarah's deeper understanding of the purposes of education, especially the kind of education we promote for people well past their schooling age years and education for kids in 4-H as a supplement to what they are learning in school.

I always felt better after these little talks with Sarah.

27
Picnic Plans

A couple of planning council members called the Extension Office before agreeing to come to the next meeting. They feared there might be another confrontation with Mike Braun. I assured them that it was unlikely, as the police chief had given him a good talking to after he learned he had no criminal record. He told him if he ever tried something like this again, he'd find himself in jail for a few days. I tried to sound confident, but I had a bad feeling that I had not seen the last of Braun. He had an inherent hatred for the government, our office, and especially me.

This time, the council met under the leadership of John Flyer, the John Deere implement dealer in Willow River. He called the meeting to order. Interestingly, he did not comment on the group doing yoga before the previous meeting, but I noticed he chose to get the group right down to business.

"Welcome back. I trust we'll not have the likes of Mike Braun scaring the bejeebers out of some of us like the last time we met." He turned toward me and smiled when he said it.

"The police chief spent a little time with Braun after our last meeting. I don't think we'll see him storming in here like he did last time," I said.

I proceeded to distribute the list of issues facing Ames County agriculture that we agreed on during the last meeting.

"Okay, any questions about what we've done so far?" asked John. "Any changes anyone wants to make to the list?" John held up a copy of what I had distributed.

Ames County Agricultural Planning Council
Ames County Agricultural Issues and Challenges
1. Irrigation and declining lake levels
2. Disagreement between industrial-size farmers and small-acreage farmers
3. Unpredictable markets and prices for farm products
4. Loss of family farms
5. Group wants to close Ext. office
6. Public doesn't know the importance of farmers
7. Water
8. Climate change
9. Rural history not well known

Hearing none, John suggested we move on. "Scott, do you have any comments?" John looked at me.

"Well, first I want to say thanks to each of you for continuing to be a part of this planning council. I know each of you has lots of other things to do. I suggest we move forward doing some of what we discussed at our very first meeting." I handed out a second sheet:

Ames County Agricultural Planning Council
Possible Activities and Events
- June Dairy Month Program
- Farm-City Picnic
- Farm History Day at Museum
- Special Activities at County Fair
- 4-H Speaking Contest
- Farm Tours
- Early Farming Stories

"I suggest a farm-city picnic," said John. "Hold it at Willow River Memorial Park, right on the lake. Invite everyone in the community to come: farmers, town folks, lake people, families, kids, grandkids, everybody. Open it up to the public. Get everybody together where they can eat, play games, listen to some music, and have fun together. Call it an "old-fashioned farm-city community picnic."

"Sounds like fun," offered Jodi. "Everybody likes a summer picnic, especially if we can have beer, bratwurst, and a polka band," she said with a big smile.

"And who is going to pay for the beer and bratwurst?" asked Jill, with a hint of skepticism in her voice.

"Tell you what," said John, "John Deere Implement will cover the cost of ice cream, beer, and soft drinks."

Bill held up his hand. "The Farm Bureau will cover the cost of the bratwurst."

Not to be outdone by his competing farm organization, Emil said, "The Farmers Union will cover the cost of all the fixin's, including potato salad and dill pickles.

"Thank you, all," I said. "Nothing will draw a crowd faster than beer and free bratwurst, with all the fixin's."

Harvey chimed in. "My brother plays tuba in a little polka band. I'll twist his arm a little, and I bet we can get him and his buddies to play for nothing. It'll be good publicity for them. Besides, they're pretty good. They call themselves the Polka Pals."

"Sounds great," said Jodi. "Beer, bratwurst, and polka music made Wisconsin what it is. At least around here. I'll get members of my group to help with frying the bratwurst and serve the beverages."

"I'll get some volunteers from my group to help as well," said Jill.

"I'll be there and help where you need me," said Jeff. "Looking forward to meeting the good people here in Ames County."

"I'll make sure the idea gets plenty of publicity," said Greg. I'll put a half-page ad in the *Gazette*, and I'll volunteer right now to be one of the brat fryers. Hate to brag in front of this auspicious group, but I'm known in certain circles as a darn good brat fryer. And, tell you what. I'll contact some of our advertisers to see if I can get some door prizes. People like door prizes."

I was elated with what I was hearing. The council unanimously accepted the farm-city picnic idea. Maybe this would be another step in healing old wounds and helping the citizens of Ames County move forward together for a change.

When the next issue of the *Gazette* arrived, Gladys dropped it on my desk and said, "Got a nice story on the front page."

"Old-Fashioned Farm-City Community Picnic"
Willow River Memorial Park,
Sunday, July 23, 11:00 a.m. to 6:00 p.m.
Free bratwurst, ice cream, and soft drinks
Beer tent
Polka Pals band

The recently organized Ames County Agricultural Planning Council is sponsoring a farm-city picnic. Everyone interested in learning more about Ames County agriculture is invited. The John Deere dealership is providing free ice cream, beer, and soft drinks. The Ames County Farm Bureau and Ames County Farmers Union are providing free bratwurst with all the trimmings. The Polka Pals, a well-known local dance band, will entertain from 2:00 to 5:00 p.m.

There will be games for the children, with prizes. Finally, there will be a wide assortment of valuable door prizes for lucky ticket holders—tickets available as people enter the picnic grounds.

Scott Olson, Ames County agricultural agent, said, "Thanks to the generous contributions of several Ames County agricultural groups, everyone living in Ames County, whether in the country or in town is invited—this includes the many folks who have cabins on Ames County's beautiful lakes. Everyone will have a chance to eat, enjoy a beverage, listen to some good old-fashioned music, and get a little better acquainted with their neighbors."

I sat back in my chair and thought, *If this works, I'll be killing two birds with one stone. Helping the non-farm folks here in the county learn a little bit about the farming that goes on here from the farmers themselves. We've got the 4-H kids making posters talking about agriculture today. The Extension Homemakers will have a booth telling what they do. Both the Farm Bureau and the Farmers Union will have booths with members sharing what they do. Getting people to talk to each other, eat bratwurst, drink a little beer, eat ice cream, and listen to polka music just might do the trick of helping people understand each other a bit better.*

It was already mid-summer, but we still had some time to plan the event and make sure everyone knew about it. Both Emil Barnes and Bill Workman planned to put notices in their monthly newsletters, besides putting information about the event on their social media. Jodi Henderson said she'd make sure the small-acreage farmers all got a personal invitation, and Jill Varsac was planning to have members of her group phone each other and email each group member. Harvey Rivers said he'd make a personal plea at their next meeting for all members to attend.

If all of this works, we could have more than a thousand people at the picnic. Wouldn't that be something? I'll invite the TV stations in Green Bay and Wausau, along with reporters from the *Wisconsin State Journal* and the *Milwaukee Journal Sentinel*.

For the first time in many days, I felt good about what was happening. I allowed the thoughts of the threatening letters to settle into the farther reaches of my memory. It did occur to me, though, that I'd better let Chief Wilkins know what we were planning so he could at least make plans for parking, traffic control, and provide a police presence.

28
Memories

Ames County Gazette
"Farm Memories from Yesterday"

As readers of the Gazette know, we are running a series of stories submitted by retired farmers about farm life in Ames County fifty-plus years ago. This week we are pleased to share a story submitted by Gladys Peterson, age eighty, who lives on a farm west of Willow River with her husband, Noel.

"The Wood-Burning Kitchen Range"
By Gladys Peterson

Let me start by saying that I have led a wonderful life, even though the challenges were many. My husband, Noel, and I raised three sons. Our oldest, Steve, and his family continue to farm on the home place. They live in a newer home just down the road from the home place where Noel and I live.

I suspect people reading this might be interested in what the job of a farm woman was back fifty or sixty years ago. Some people like to call that time "The Good Old Days." Compared to today's hurry-up, get it done as quick as possible attitude, we were not in a hurry. We couldn't be, even if we wanted to. We had no electricity, no indoor plumbing, and I did all our cooking and baking on a wood stove. People today would have you believe that cooking on a wood stove was the most wonderful thing.

Well, it wasn't. Wood-burning stoves are messy. There are ashes to carry out every day. There is wood to carry in every day. And there is lots of dirt and dust. Sometimes I was pleased that we had no electricity as a kerosene lamp doesn't offer much light, especially when compared to electric light bulbs. I mention this because, with the meager light from a kerosene lamp, visitors could not see all the dust that accumulates when burning wood.

I learned from my mother how to cook on a wood stove. But before I say more, let me describe what one looked like. The left side of the stove, with four round lids, covered the firebox where you put the wood. A little to the right and down was the oven, with a big door that opened and offered a place for someone to warm his stocking feet on a cold day in winter. A little farther to the right was a section of the stove, which held several gallons of water. It's called the reservoir, and it was our source of warm water for cooking and for washing our hands and faces. Hot water came from the ever-present teakettle on the stove.

The warming oven was about eighteen inches above the stovetop. As the name suggests, it was a place to keep things warm. A stove pipe came out of the back of the stove and stuck into the chimney that led to the roof. Occasionally, when the wind was in the north and rather brisk, it would send oak smoke down the chimney and into the kitchen. I must say, I always rather enjoyed the smell of wood smoke but did not appreciate it when the wind drove the smoke into my kitchen. When the wind did that, we knew that a storm was brewing. One more way that we were able to predict the weather.

The ashtray was under the firebox. Each morning before starting the fire in the stove—that was Noel's job—he pulled out the ashtray and dumped the ashes on the ash pile a few steps from the kitchen's backdoor. By the way, many folks don't know that hardwood ashes contain lots of potash. Every spring, Noel would fork the contents of the ash pile into the manure spreader and spread it on our potato patch. For potatoes to grow well, they require lots of potash.

We had twenty acres of mostly oak trees growing to the north of our farm buildings, so we had an ample supply of oak wood for the cook stove as well as for the dining room heater and the stove in the pump house that kept the water pump from freezing on below-zero mornings. It seemed we could expect below-zero mornings from about early November to the first week in March. Sometimes the temperature crept clear down to thirty-five and even forty-below. Brr.

It took a fair amount of skill to cook with a wood-burning cook stove. First off, the stove had no thermometer. I learned from my mother how to judge when the stove was hot enough to cook various things. For instance, when I would fry something in the cast-iron skillet, say fresh pork chops, I put the skillet on the hottest part of the stove and then drop in a little water. If a drop of water sizzled and bounced, I knew the skillet was ready. When baking bread, I learned from Ma how to open the oven door a little and put my hand in to determine if the heat was right for baking.

Another thing I learned about cooking with wood was to identify the different kinds of wood, and to put them in the stove to regulate the heat. For instance, pine wood burns fast but not very hot. Oak wood burns hotter and more slowly. As the old-timers would say, "Oak wood holds the heat." Of course, pine kindling—pine cut into little pieces—worked well to start the fire.

Our kitchen wood stove, which had a fire in it all days of the year, no matter if it was twenty-below or ninety in the shade, was where I cooked and baked and where I canned vegetables, meat, and fruit and heated water for clothes washing. I have many pleasant memories of that old stove and, to be honest, many that were not so pleasant.

29
Fred and Oscar

"So Fred, have you heard about the big farm-city picnic coming up next month?" asked Oscar Anderson.

"Yeah, I read about it," said Fred.

"You don't sound too excited."

"Oh, I'm excited. I do like the idea of free beer, ice cream, and bratwurst. Hard to find much that's free these days," said Fred.

"So, you don't think it's a good idea to get people together to learn a little more about the farming in Ames County these days?" asked Oscar.

"Thought that's what we were doing when you and I wrote those articles for the *Gazette* a while back."

"Fred, how we farmed fifty years ago is not how farming is done today. I think you know that," said Oscar, motioning for the waitress to refill his coffee cup. "It's important that folks know what farming was like yesterday, but we'd all better know something about how it's done today."

"Expect you're right. But what happens when people learn a bit more about farming and then decide they don't like what they're finding out? What then?" A serious look spread across Fred's usually jovial face.

"But isn't it worse if people don't know what's going on? Especially those who don't live on farms. I hate to say this, but some of them just don't care what happens down on the farm as long as they've got a steady supply of safe, cheap food," said Oscar.

"Does get kind of complicated, doesn't it?" said Fred.

"It does," said Oscar. "But I hand it to our county agent, Scott Olson. He's trying to get people to understand what's going on these days. He's got his hands full."

"I guess the picnic is a good idea. Get people knowing each other," said Fred.

"Well, are you going, Fred? To the picnic?"

"I expect I will. I really don't like big crowds. Could be a lot of folks after that free beer, ice cream, and brats. Kinda glad we ain't farming anymore. I remember when I quit. We were milkin' forty cows and thought that was a lot," said Fred, sipping his coffee.

"Remember that big pushback starting back in the seventies and still goin' on today—get bigger or get out? Remember that?" asked Oscar.

"I sure do. Banks were lending money to farmers by the thousands of dollars, implement dealers were selling more tractors and big combines and forage harvesters and other stuff than they could keep on their lots. And then you know what happened?" asked Fred.

"I sure do. The 2007 recession came along, and we had a farm crisis near as bad as the Great Depression. Across this country thousands of farmers lost their farms to bankruptcy. Many farm auctions were held. A terrible time. Farmers got too big too fast. That's what happened." Oscar rubbed his hand through his gray hair.

"I remember those years well. Lots of crying and hand wringing. It was a terrible time. I went to some of those auctions. Women crying, men with big, calloused hands and sloping shoulders watching their life work sold by a fast-talking auctioneer, the greedy bankers, many who helped cause the problem, standing by to claim the bankrupt land. Glad I decided to stay small. Sure glad of that. I may not have been making much money, but at least I had my farm. Had my land," said Fred.

Both men sat quietly, remembering those awful years from 2007 to 2009.

"Hope we're not going in that same direction today," said Oscar. "When is big too big? Agriculture has a tough time with that question. Farmers are compared to industrialists these days, but comparison doesn't work. The industrialist makes something, say a refrigerator. Well, some bad times come along and few people are buying refrigerators. What does the refrigerator maker do during tough economic times? He lays off some workers, stores his refrigerators, and when times pick up he's back in business. On the other hand, what a farmer produces mostly can't be stored—milk especially. After a few days, it goes bad. Same for fresh fruits and vegetables. Once they are harvested, unless somebody buys them in a few days, they rot. It's a big problem. Always has been. Marketing farm produce is very complicated."

"That's a pretty fancy speech you've got there, Oscar."

"Nothing fancy about it at all. It's just the way it works. You can't compare what a farmer does to what an industrialist does. Some folks want to call these large farms 'factory farms.' There's no such thing as a factory farm. Farms are not factories. The sooner we learn that, the better off we'll all be."

"You got more, Oscar? You seem to be windin' up pretty good on this topic."

"I've got lot's more to say about this, Fred. Been thinking about it for a long time. Haven't even begun to talk about these big farms and taking care of the land and water so the next generation will have something to work with. Could talk about that for a long time."

"But you're gonna spare me today, I hope?" said Fred.

"Anyway, you goin' to this Farm-City picnic?" asked Oscar.

"I sure am," said Fred. "Isn't every day I can have a free beer and a brat and a chance to listen to polka music. Besides, Harvey Rivers from the historical society asked if I'd sit in his booth and talk with folks about threshing days—especially folks who read my story in the *Gazette*." Fred was feeling pretty good that he'd be able to hold back this information from his old friend and then surprise him with it.

"Guess what?" said Oscar, with a big smile spreading across his wrinkled face.

"What?" said Fred.

"I'm gonna be sitting right next to you. Harvey asked me to bring along an old barn lantern and talk to folks about lamps and lanterns—especially folks who read MY article in the *Gazette*."

"Well, what do you know about that," was all Fred could think to say.

30
Chickens and the Garden

Ames County Gazette

Here is another story submitted to the Gazette on the topic of Ames County agriculture fifty-plus years ago. This one was sent in by octogenarian Mable Lucas, who farmed with her husband north of Link Lake.

"Garden and Chickens"
By Mable Lucas

My memory is not as good as it once was, but I've managed to remember quite well when my husband, Frederick, farmed. We raised three children. We'd hoped one of them would stay on the farm, but all three moved away once they completed their educations.

I wrote down a few thoughts about what farm women typically did in my generation on the farm. Our farm was 160 acres, the common size for many farms in Ames County at the time. At the most, we milked about twenty cows, and that was when we got electricity after World War II and could afford to buy a milking machine.

Frederick was in charge of the cows, the hogs, and the fieldwork. I was responsible for the chickens and the garden. Of course, I also did all the cooking and baking, dealt with the kids' cuts and bruises, and helped them with their schoolwork, all while doing the mending and clothes washing and ironing.

Now the chickens. We always had about a hundred layers. White Leghorns, they were. The chicken house was just west of the main house, so it didn't take me long to get there—and I was there three times a day and more. Feeding, watering, and gathering eggs.

Once a week, on Saturday, when we went to town for groceries, I took several dozen eggs along and traded them for groceries at the Link Lake Mercantile. I usually had a few dollars left over, and I put the money in a little jar I kept in the cupboard. I used that money to buy things from the Watkins man when he visited about once a month. That money also bought clothes and shoes for the kids, plus birthday and Christmas presents. Sometimes, when the hens were really laying good, I'd have enough eggs left over from my grocery trading to sell to the egg man who came by the farm every two weeks or so.

I could tell about some of the troubles we had. One time, a fox got into the henhouse and made off with a couple hens. Another time, a weasel snuck in and killed several of my best layers. But I'd rather say that the chickens did well over the years, and I got along with them just fine. Though sometimes things looked pretty bleak when some critter got into the chicken house and killed a bunch of them.

My other big project was the vegetable garden, starting in January when I ordered the seeds from a seed catalog to March when I planted the cabbage and tomato seeds, to mid-April when Frederick plowed the garden spot and marked the rows for me. He and the kids helped me plant a few rows of early potatoes, peas, lettuce, radishes, carrots, and onions (I bought the onion sets at the mercantile). We'd also set out the cabbage plants I'd started from seed.

We'd wait until late May to set out the tomato plants. I saved old empty coffee cans to put around each tomato plant to keep away the cutworms and protect the frail little plants from chilly nights that occasionally still came around in late May. About the time we set out the tomato plants, we also planted the *green beans, sweet corn, beets, and rutabagas. Frederick liked rutabagas, so we always had a row of them.*

As June rolled around, we usually ate freshly pulled radishes and lettuce. It was like a taste of spring to eat those fresh vegetables. By mid-summer we were eating new red potatoes, the first early tomatoes, green beans, and some of the early sweet corn. And then sliced cucumbers. We felt so lucky to have all of these fresh vegetables and just a hop and skip from the back door of the kitchen.

By late summer, I was up to my elbows in canning vegetables. I canned everything from green beans to dill pickles, carrots to sweet corn. As soon as we got electricity, we bought a freezer, which made my life a lot easier. I don't recall in all the years we lived on the farm, that I once bought a vegetable. If we didn't grow it, we didn't eat it.

31
Farm-City Picnic

I climbed into my truck at seven o'clock on the Sunday morning we'd picked for our big farm-city picnic and drove slowly to the park only a few blocks from my apartment. It was a picture-perfect day. Not a cloud in the deep blue sky. A slight breeze rippled the waters of Ames Lake. When I arrived at the park, I saw members of the planning council setting up for the picnic. I had my fingers crossed that nothing would disturb the event, building on our great success with the June Dairy Month Breakfast.

Chief Wilkins wasn't taking any chances. With a temporary fence, he organized the entrance to the picnic grounds so that everyone had to pass through the same gate. He would have one of his officers do a visual check of everyone coming to the picnic. The chief had also told me that all of his officers would be on duty at the picnic, several of them in plain clothes. He seemed more concerned about something bad happening than I did; maybe he had heard something that put him on high alert—something he hadn't told me. I decided I would let the chief worry about security and, along with Sarah, the two of us would do our best to make this picnic a success.

Sarah had gotten to the park ahead of me and was busy working with the Ames County Homemakers to organize a booth that told about the group's history, what they had accomplished over the years, and what their program plans were for this year. Her big smile when I approached always brightened my day.

"Good morning, Scott," she said. "Great day for a picnic."

"That it is. You need any help here?"

"Nope. I think we've got it all under control," Sarah said. "Two of our longtime Homemaker members, Gladys and Mable, are helping. I'm sure you saw the articles they wrote for the *Gazette* about the work farm women had to do in the early days."

"So nice to see both of you," I said. "And congratulations on those articles. Very nicely done. I remember being on Mable's farm several years ago."

"Yes, you were. Must have been about eight years ago—you should stop out and chat again sometime. I know Frederick would especially like it. He's not very well these days. Seldom gets out of the house."

"Sorry to hear that," I said, putting in my mental notebook that I should plan a visit to the Lucas farm in the near future.

As part of the council's planning for the picnic, we had agreed that any agricultural group that wanted to put up a booth, should do so. It would be a good chance to show off the various aspects of Ames County's agriculture to the public. I saw a line of booths. Next to the Homemakers' booth was one devoted to 4-H club work in Ames County. Sarah helped some of the older 4-H members put that booth together. Featured in the display were various 4-H projects and an invitation for girls and boys, ages eight to eighteen, to join whether they lived in the country or in town. Younger children, ages five to seven, could become cloverbud members. Featured in the booth was a live rabbit, a project for one of the members in the booth.

I spotted Aimee Johnson, who was in charge of the games for the little kids that came by. One game she had set up included old milk bottles. The idea of the game was to toss a ring over one of the bottles. The winner received a 4-H flag with the organization's motto: "To make the best better." I didn't see Josh Henderson. I felt badly that just because Aimee's father didn't agree with Josh's family's approach to farming, the two young people couldn't see each other.

Walking on, I came to a booth with large blue words: "WATER IN OUR FUTURE." There I met a smiling Jill Varsac.

"Nice booth," I said when I approached.

"I'm glad you think so," she said. Before we'd organized the Agricultural Planning Council, I had not met Jill but had read some of her often rather strident statements that she regularly made to the media. She was making me think of water in new ways. I don't know what some of the other council members thought of her, especially people like Jesse Johnson, who operated several deep-well pumps that sprayed millions of gallons of water on his vegetable crops. But I must say, I have developed a considerable respect for the young woman. I don't always agree with her strategy, but when she shares information, it is well-researched and accurate—I've checked.

Harvey Rivers and several historical society members put together a collection of old farming equipment, especially the tools farmers used during the years before electricity arrived on the farm. I saw a cradle, the scythe-like tool that was used to cut grain before reapers and binders became popular. I saw several woodworking tools—a broad ax that had been used to hew logs into timbers used for barn construction, a hand-operated drill, and a drawshave for smoothing lumber.

On either side of the exhibit, I saw Oscar Anderson and Fred Russo, two old farmers I had known for several years. I shook their hands and complimented them on the articles of early-day farming in the *Gazette*. I couldn't have been more pleased with the suggestion for stories from early farming in Ames County.

I glanced back at the Ames County Historical Society's booth and saw several people talking with Oscar and Fred about what they remembered about their early life on the farm. It was shaping up to be the kind of day I had hoped for.

Next was the bratwurst grill as I continued my tour of the picnic grounds. I saw John Flyer working with Jeff Miles and Jill Varsac. What a great way for the three of them—a businessman, a loan officer, and the head of an environmental group—to become better acquainted.

I could tell they had been on duty for some time as the charcoal was a hot, dull gray, and the first brats were lined up, sizzling and sending off that wonderful smell of meat cooking on a charcoal grill.

I stopped to chat for a few minutes with the three of them.

"Ready for a brat?" John asked, reaching for a bun with one hand and giant tongs with the other.

"No, a little too early," I said. "But you'll have customers soon—I saw the first families coming through the gate."

"We're ready," said Jill. "We've got lots of brats, so the more people, the better."

The next two booths represented the Farm Bureau and the Farmers Union, both staffed by members who were ready to chat with whoever came by about each of the organizations. I thought it interesting that the organizations had erected booths adjacent to each other. Each booth featured information about farming in Ames County today with photos and descriptions of modern dairy barns, photos of vast corn and soybean fields, and some pictures of irrigation sweeps working in enormous vegetable fields.

So far, I didn't see any action at the beer tent, but that would soon change as the day was becoming warmer, and the smell of fried bratwurst was wafting across the picnic grounds.

Jodi Henderson and her small-acreage farm group had a booth with photos of several of the small-acreage farm vegetable fields. I stopped by to chat with Jodi and recognized Don Lathrop and his family. I was pleased to see them.

"Don, Jane," I said. "How's it going? Good to see you again. How are these two little ones? Let's see, their names are Constance and Ben."

"You have a good memory," Jane said.

"Thanks for suggesting we get in touch with Jodi," Don said. "If I knew half of what this woman knows about vegetable growing, we'd be in great shape."

Jodi smiled. "Thank you. Best way to learn this business is to get your hands dirty, and you two seem interested in doing that."

It was now ten o'clock, and the Polka Pals were tuning up on a little covered stage that was part of the park complex. A big sign adorned the front of the stage. Their band consisted of a tuba player, an accordion player, a woman playing trumpet and sax, plus a fellow playing guitar and singing.

"Welcome, everyone," the guitar player said. Huge speakers had been erected on either side of the stage, so the sound of the fellow's voice carried throughout the picnic area. "We're the Polka Pals, and we'll be here all day playing your favorite polkas, old-time waltzes, and even old-time, sometimes forgotten music that the old-timers in the crowd will remember."

The band immediately began playing "In the Good Old Summertime." It had been years since I'd heard that tune. Then it was "Happy Days Are Here Again." I saw people lining up at the brat stand and the beer tent, and families were claiming picnic tables near the bandstand so they could be closer to the music.

But then I heard loud talking at the entrance gate, and several police officers were hurrying in that direction. I hurried there as well.

32
Gunshots at the Picnic

When I arrived at the entrance gate, I saw a police officer holding up his hand to stop a group of men wearing bright red shirts that had emblazoned on them an image of a bald eagle with an arrow in one talon and a silver dollar in the other, and the words "Eagle Party: For the People." I spotted Mike Braun at the head of the group, and behind him I saw Paul Workman, Bill's son. I counted ten men altogether, and they looked like trouble.

I also glimpsed Chief Wilkins running toward the gate with a very concerned look on his face. The police officer at the gate held his ground, no doubt having gotten strict instructions from Chief Wilkins to not let anyone into the picnic who might disrupt the event.

"We've every right to be here," said a red-faced Mike Braun as he pointed a long finger at the chest of the police officer. "We are taxpaying American citizens," he said in a raised voice.

"What are your intentions?" asked the officer, who obviously had not encountered Braun and his group previously.

"That, young man, is none of your business. We are members of the Eagle Political Party, as you can plainly see, and we know our rights as citizens. We have a right to attend this picnic along with everyone else," Braun shouted.

In the background, I heard the band playing polka music. I saw a long line at the brat stand and an equally long line at the beer tent. I saw a group of kids playing some game that Aimee Johnson had organized. A cluster of old-timers chatted with Oscar and Fred, no doubt reminiscing about farming in the early days.

Chief Wilkins arrived at the entrance gate at the same time I did.

"What's going on here?" the chief asked, a bit out of breath. "What are you doing here, Mr. Braun? Can't you see that this is a peaceful picnic?"

I stood off to the side. Braun looked at me with a sneer on his face. I noticed that Chief Wilkins was giving Braun the once over, looking for weapons.

"You wouldn't mind if I patted you down to make sure you aren't carrying, as you were the other day in the Extension Office."

"You just pat away," said Braun, lifting his arms high over his head.

Finding nothing, I heard the chief ask again, "What are you doing here?"

"We heard this picnic was open to everyone, and we thought we'd come by for some free brats and maybe a beer," said Braun.

"What about those signs I see you guys carrying?" asked the chief.

"Oh, you've noticed the signs," Braun said sarcastically. "Maybe we plan on holding them up from time to time when we are eating and drinking. Give folks a chance to see what they say."

Chief Wilkins paused for a bit and noticed a long line behind Braun and his followers, waiting to get onto the picnic grounds.

"Okay, you guys can come in. But if I notice that you're causing any kind of disruption, out you go. I'll ask one of my officers to tag along with you."

"Why the hell for?" Braun said.

"Well, to be brutally frank, to make sure you are a man of your word and to make sure someone doesn't decide to take a swing at one of you guys."

"Geez," Braun said as he motioned to his group to follow him onto the picnic grounds, each holding his big red Eagle Party sign high. They walked about six feet apart, and a few people turned to look at them, but most folks were too busy eating, drinking, and listening to the music to pay much attention to ten guys wearing red shirts and holding big signs.

I knew Chief Wilkins had to let them in; they have a right to protest. But I also know that this group wants to close down my office and most other government offices. I watched them march around for fifteen minutes or so and began relaxing. Most people ignored them, although seeing protestors carrying big signs was unusual. Folks saw that in the big cities, not out here in little rural Ames County.

I walked over to chat with Sarah at the Homemakers' booth. Both Gladys and Mable were chatting with a group of older women, no doubt comparing notes on what farm life for women was like fifty years ago. Along with the older women, I also saw several young girls listening and asking questions of Gladys and Mable, doing exactly what I hoped would happen at this picnic.

I noticed that Jill's booth on water had attracted considerable attention. She shared the booth with George Emerson. I'd like to have been a mouse in the corner to have heard what they talked about between visits with people who stopped by their booth to chat.

I also thought about Jesse Johnson and his huge irrigated vegetable operation west of here. I noticed he was working in the Farm Bureau booth, handing out brochures to people interested in learning more about that organization.

"Jill," I said when I caught her attention, "has Jesse stopped by your booth?"

"He walked by, said a quick hello, and then walked on. I don't think he saw much of what we have here," she said.

I saw Chief Wilkins strolling by. He looked the most relaxed that I'd seen him all day.

"How are things going, Chief?" I asked.

"Just peachy," he said with a big smile. "Those Eagle Party guys are behaving themselves as they promised. Plenty of brats and beer, and the weather is just perfect for doing anything outside."

I was enjoying the moment as well. A huge crowd was having a good time, and I believe learning a bit more about farming yesterday and something about what it was like today.

Then the chief and I both heard it at the same time. *Bang ... Bang ... Bang ... Bang.* The chief was immediately on full alert. He had his radio out, and he was yelling into it, "Gunshots near the lake. Gunshots near the lake." He began running toward the little wooden shelter where the restrooms were located a hundred yards away and near the lake.

Almost immediately I saw a police cruiser wending its way through the crowd, its siren blaring. Most people had heard the shots as well. I wondered what was next. Was this the beginning of a disaster with some crazy person shooting into the crowd? Could it be one of those Eagle Party members who somehow got through the entry gate with a weapon? Some of them had violent tendencies; I saw that firsthand with my encounter with Mike. Was it the person who had thrown the rock through the window with a threatening letter and the same person who mailed me the second letter who was doing the shooting? Were those gunshots meant for me?

I ran to Sarah's booth to see if she was okay. She was, but she was white as a sheet. Obviously, she was very concerned about hearing the gunshots.

"What should we do?" she said, trying not to speak too loudly.

"I don't know. The police estimate there must be five hundred people here today, and I'm guessing that most of them heard the shots."

33

Disrupted Picnic

Police Chief Wilkins made the decision for us. He was on the stage. The polka band stopped playing, and the chief took the microphone.

"Could I have everyone's attention, please," he said in a loud, clear voice. "I must ask that everyone exit the picnic grounds as promptly as possible. My officers are opening all the exits for your use. Please leave in an orderly manner."

I knew it would happen, and having been in and around crowds of people all my career, it happened again. I saw people scooping up their children and running toward the nearest exit. There was panic. Someone bumped into Jill's booth and it went crashing to the ground. The crew cooking bratwurst were dumping bottles of beer on the hot coals, trying to extinguish them before they rushed for the exits.

The band did not leave but continued to play one polka after another and then a series of old-time waltzes. But people were not listening to the music; they were listening for more gunshots, looking over their shoulders for someone with a gun.

In less than half an hour the picnic grounds were empty of people, except for the polka band and a handful of the planning council members who had remained along with Sarah and me.

"I told the polka people they could quit playing," Chief Wilkins said when he walked up to me.

"You find the shooter?" I asked, concerned that the culprit might still be in the area.

"We did not," said the chief. "He must have joined the crowd that left. No way we could spot him in that mass of scared people running for the exits."

The once neat and tidy picnic grounds were a mess. I saw paper plates scattered everywhere, torn and bent Eagle Party signs, beer bottles tossed here and there, broken booths, torn canvas, tipped-over picnic tables, a couple of Milwaukee Brewers caps crumpled in the dust.

"Was anybody shot?" I asked, thinking the shots may have been intended for me.

"Not that we could tell. We found no signs of blood, no report from anyone of gunshot wounds. A few people were hurt. People in a panic tend to hurt others. Nothing serious, though. My officers saw some scrapes and bruises, one bloody nose. I think we have everything under control," the chief said, breathing a big sigh of relief.

I should have taken a minute to tell Chief Wilkins how much I appreciated what he did, but frankly, I was still in shock. I had so much looked forward to this picnic being a success, and it turned out to be just the opposite. How could we invite people to any future events without them thinking they would be in danger if they attended?

Was this all about me? Maybe I'm becoming a little paranoid, but maybe the shots weren't just to disrupt the picnic but a personal warning to me—another kind of message following the two letters I had already received.

I mentioned all of this to Sarah as I helped her pack up what was left of her tattered booth. I shouldn't have.

"Scott," she said, with the most serious look I had ever seen on her face. "This is just awful what happened today. Just awful. What are you gonna do?"

"I don't know," I said. I could feel a huge headache developing just above my eyes. "Good thing that Chief Wilkins and his officers were here."

"Didn't help the panic much. I thought the polka band might help. I remember how the band kept playing when the *Titanic* sank. Calmed down some of the people," Sarah said.

"Sure didn't calm down these folks. All they wanted was to get out of here as fast as they could. Couldn't blame them. Hear gunshots, and it's human nature to run away as quickly as possible."

"Scott, come over to my place for supper this evening. We've got to talk."

"Okay," I said, rubbing my aching head.

My headache worsened when I arrived at Sarah's cabin. She was busy preparing supper when I arrived, trying to be her usual upbeat self, but she couldn't hide her concerns.

"How are you feeling?" she asked, though she could quickly see that I was as despondent as she had ever seen me, and we had been together for many years.

"What a catastrophe," I mumbled, rubbing my aching head. "What a complete disaster." I held my head in my hands as Sarah began rubbing my neck.

"What are you going to do?" she asked.

"I don't know. I just don't know. I felt so good after the dairy breakfast. I thought we were on our way to having folks talking to and getting better acquainted with each other. It's that damn Eagle Party. They're behind all of this. I'll bet one of those guys fired the shots."

"Do you think they were shooting at you?" Sarah asked as a huge frown line grew on her forehead.

"I don't know. If they were, why didn't they hit me?" I said with a weak smile.

"Scott, this is not funny. Not a bit funny. I think you are in real danger. Somebody, maybe Mike Braun's group, maybe somebody else, is really out to get you."

"Looks that way, doesn't it?" is all I could think to say. I continued to rub my head.

"Scott, you've got to make a decision." Sarah looked at me solemnly.

"The decision is made," I said. "We've got to move on. Got to figure out some approach. Can't let something like this stop us. Just can't."

"Scott, you are not making sense. No sense at all. You keep doing this stuff, putting on these events, and you'll get yourself killed. I think you should look for another job. Leave this place behind."

"Aren't you being a little overdramatic?" I said, looking up at her. "My job is to help people, and I'm trying my best to do that."

"I am not being overdramatic!" Sarah said each word loudly and clearly. Her face was red, and she was pointing a finger at me.

"You are a stubborn fool. That's what you are. A stubborn fool," Sarah said as she began to sob. "Don't you ever think of me? Think of what I feel? All you have on your mind are the damn people of Ames County. Don't I count for anything?"

"Sarah, Sarah. What are you saying?"

"I'm saying you are a damn fool. That's what I'm saying. A damn fool who puts his work ahead of everything else. Especially the people who care most about you. I come in second place." She rubbed the tears from her eyes.

"Well, I guess I know where I stand," I said, pushing back my chair and standing up. "I'd best leave. I can't remember the last time somebody called me a damn fool. Sounds worse than being shot at, especially coming from you, Sarah." I quietly closed the door when I left. I could hear Sarah sobbing as I walked to my pickup.

Returning to my apartment, I left a message on Gladys's phone at the office that I would be taking a couple of days' vacation and that I would be in on Wednesday. I had to spend some time alone, thinking, considering, not thinking, dealing with my world that had fallen apart. What should I do? What could I do? Jump in my truck and drive? Drive until I am a thousand miles from here? I could do that. I've known people to do that. Maybe drive to Alaska. Find some work there. Leave this mess behind. Start over. Get past feeling that I'm a loser. A loser in my work. A loser in my relationships. A complete loser. Try something where I can be a winner for a change. So I can feel good again. Feeling that I can go on living. Feel good about myself.

34
Firecrackers

I was at my desk promptly at eight on Wednesday morning. I did not feel good, but I was feeling better than I had Sunday evening when my world collapsed around me. I still had a headache but nothing like the one I had Sunday evening. All I could think about for the past two days was Sarah and how I had messed up everything in our relationship. I shouldn't have walked out on her. I should have listened to her. She surely has a point. For the last few months, all that I've done is worry about bringing people with different points of view together to help them better understand each other. And right in front of my nose, I can't even work out my relationship with Sarah. I can't even take the time to hear her out and understand her perspective. What a fool I've been.

I heard a quiet knock on the door, and Gladys entered with the most recent copy of the *Ames County Gazette*, which she handed to me. "Sorry about what happened, Scott," she said as she turned to leave.

On the front page, I read:

"Gunshots End Farm-City Picnic"

Gunshots abruptly brought to an end the farm-city picnic held last Sunday at Willow River Memorial Park in Willow River. Some five hundred people attended the event, enjoying free bratwurst, ice cream, and beverages. They visited several booths about Ames County agriculture yesterday, today, and tomorrow while listening to polka music. Then they heard gunshots.

Police Chief Wilkins said, "We did what was necessary to prevent bloodshed and possible loss of life. We asked people to leave the picnic grounds promptly. Unfortunately, some people panicked, causing a few minor injuries and some property damage." The chief added, "So far we have not found the shooter, but we have an ongoing investigation."

Scott Olson, Ames County agricultural agent, who is working with the recently organized Ames County Agricultural Planning Council, said, "I am saddened by what happened today. The planning council had recently sponsored a very successful dairy breakfast, and we all had high hopes that this event might build on the success of that event. I don't know where we go from here."

This reporter attended the picnic, heard the gunshots, and witnessed the panic that ensued when people were asked to leave the picnic grounds. As Chief Wilkins said, "In all of my years as police chief in Willow River, I've never witnessed anything like this. I hope the shooter will turn him or herself in so we can bring some closure to this unfortunate incident."

I put down the paper, opened my desk drawer, and searched for the aspirin bottle I knew was there. The phone rang loudly, not helping my headache.

"Hello, this is Scott Olson," I said, trying my best to sound professional.

"Scott, this Chief Wilkins. How are you?"

"If the truth be known, not very good. I'm still thinking about the disaster on Sunday."

"I have some good news for you. The shooter on Sunday wasn't a shooter at all."

"Not a shooter," I mumbled, not understanding what the chief was getting at.

"A mother and her fourteen-year-old son just left my office. The mother read the paper and knew that her son had gotten some illegal firecrackers from a friend—big firecrackers that sounded a lot like gunshots. She dragged her son down to my office, and he confessed the whole thing. He set off the firecrackers behind the restroom and then disappeared into the crowd."

"Really," was all I could think to say.

"The kid said he was sorry. He only wanted to see how people might react—and I guess he found out."

"You mean we scared five hundred people into running away from four firecrackers?"

"That's about the size of it," the chief said. "Wish we had known sooner that they weren't gunshots. We could have told the audience, and everything would have gone on as normal."

"Geez, Chief. What next?"

"I'll call Greg Charter at the *Gazette* and let him know. I'll also call the TV folks in Green Bay and the Link Lake radio station. People need to know that we don't have an active shooter running around Ames County."

"Thanks for letting me know." I hung up the phone and sat back in my chair. My first thought was, *At least no one was shooting at me.*

I heard Sarah arrive while I was on the phone and decided I should immediately tell her and Gladys what really happened at the picnic.

Sarah was chatting with Gladys when I came from my office. It was the first time in several days that I felt like smiling.

"I have news," I said. I was carrying the *Gazette* with me. "There was no shooter at the picnic on Sunday."

"What do you mean, no shooter?" Sarah said. "I heard the shots just like everyone else did."

"I just got off the phone with Chief Wilkins, and what sounded like shots were really firecrackers."

"Firecrackers?" Sarah said.

"Big firecrackers that some kid had gotten illegally and set them off behind the restrooms last Sunday. The kid's mother and the kid stopped by the chief's office this morning after she'd read this story in the paper." I held up the newspaper with the story.

"You mean all that panic and mess was caused by firecrackers?" Gladys said.

"That's about it," I said. "Chief Wilkins may have overreacted a little, but I'm not going to tell him that. I remember my mother saying, 'Better to be safe than sorry.'"

"What a mess," Sarah said. "What a mess."

I wanted to say something to Sarah, but not in front of Gladys. And besides, Sarah was showing her professional side. I was still wondering if she thought I was the jerk she had said I was on Sunday evening. I've got to figure out a way to talk with her.

"So, what do we do about the Ames County Agricultural Planning Council?" Sarah asked, this time looking at me.

"I really don't know. Got any ideas?"

35
Fred and Oscar

"That picnic on Sunday was really something," said Fred as he sat across from his old friend, Oscar. They were enjoying their breakfasts at the Black Oak Café in Link Lake.

"You read the *Gazette* this morning?" Oscar asked. He had a copy with him.

"Yup, I did," said Fred. "Story was pretty bland compared to what really happened. I about wet my pants when I heard them gunshots."

"Really," said Oscar, smiling.

"Surprised myself, I did. Didn't know I could move so fast. If it weren't for the covey of Eagle Party guys stumbling along and trying to keep track of their fancy signs, I'd been outta there even sooner. How about you, Oscar? I didn't see which direction you ran?"

"Ran out the back, along the lake. Less people there. You listen to the Link Lake radio station this morning?"

"I did not," said Fred. "I like my mornings to be peaceful. I like the quiet. No radio. No TV. Just the quiet."

"Then, I bet I know something that you don't," said Oscar as he picked up his coffee cup.

"And that would be?" asked Fred.

"There were no gunshots at the picnic."

"What do you mean there were no gunshots? I heard 'em loud and clear, just like everybody else," said Fred. "Those surely were gunshots I heard."

"Firecrackers, Fred. Those were big firecrackers going off."

"How'd you know that?"

"Heard it on the Link Lake radio station. They quoted Chief Wilkins, who said a fourteen-year-old kid fessed up that he set off the big firecrackers."

"Well, I'll be damned," said Fred. "All that fuss and mess over firecrackers."

"That's what it was—big old firecrackers that this kid had gotten somewhere, and he thought the picnic might be a good place to set them off. Chief said the kid had wanted to impress people with his big firecrackers. He impressed them all right. Raised particular hell with the Willow River Memorial Park and messed up a good picnic. I never got to finish my brat and beer," said Oscar.

"Neither did I, dammit. Pretty good brat it was, too. And you can't beat Point Special beer. Dang good stuff."

"Wonder if that planning council will be puttin' on another shindig like Sunday. Thought they had a pretty good idea, with them booths showing what farming was like yesterday and today, and all the free food. Big crowd, too," said Oscar holding up his coffee so the waitress could give him a refill.

"Yeah, it was kinda fun sittin' in the historical society booth and chatting with folks about what farm life was like when we were kids. Surprised how many people are interested in that. Really surprised how many kids wanted to talk with us," said Fred. "Sometimes the kids seem more interested than their parents."

"Just too damn bad the whole event nearly turned into a riot with everybody trying to get away from the place. Just too damn bad," said Oscar.

"What you make of them polka players? They just kept right on playin' when everybody else was running away."

"Impressed me, they did," said Oscar. "They tried to calm everybody down. But it didn't work. Gunshots scare the hell out of people. People hear about that all the time in the big cities, and when gunshots come to the country—well, people panic."

"Too bad," said Fred. "Just too damn bad that's how the picnic turned out. The county agent and that planning council had a good idea—to get city people and farm folks together, talking to each other. These groups don't know much about each other these days. Funny how that has worked out. When I was a kid, everybody knew about farmers and farming. Almost everybody, anyway. Today, well what is it? About 2 percent of the folks living in this country live on farms. And the connections of town to country just aren't there like they once were. And besides, there's squabbling among the rural people as well, little farmers and big farmers not understanding each other."

36
New Picnic Plans

I sat in my office mulling over everything that had happened since the community center incident. And the second threatening letter in the mail. These matters continued to nag at me. But mostly I was thinking about Sarah and whether our special relationship had ended. Surely, she had lost her temper with me, and for good reason, as I think about it. And, as I think about what happened Sunday night, I should not have walked out on her. I can't get out of my head the sound of her sobbing when I left her house. If I were to do it over again, I would have sat down and talked with her and allowed her to get all her feelings out on the table. I should have told her how much I loved her and how we could work things out. But no, what did I do? I got up, walked to the door, and left like an idiot. So many times in this life I had wished for a do-over. Boy, this was one of those times. But as my dad would say when something like this happened: The horse is out of the barn. You can't go back. But what should I do? Sarah would be coming into the office shortly. Should I say anything? Or should I just go on as if nothing had happened? I really don't think she wants our relationship to end—but maybe that's my ego talking—maybe she does. Maybe she wants to move on.

I never thought how much I would miss her suppers, our long discussions over glasses of wine, and the nights we spent together in her little cabin on Ames Lake.

The ringing of the phone brought me back to the present. I picked it up.

"It's George Emerson from the Winter Lake Property Owners Association on line two," Gladys said.

"Did he say what he wanted?"

"He did not," Gladys replied.

"Okay. Put him through." I took a moment before taking his call. "This is Scott Olson," I said.

"Scott, this is George Emerson. How you doing after that scare at the park on Sunday?"

"Oh, pretty good considering. I was hoping it would have turned out better."

"I suspect we all were," George said.

"Our planning council put a lot of time and effort into planning that picnic, and I'm not sure what came of it beyond scaring a lot of people to death," I said.

"Scott, don't be too hard on yourself. I've been talking with some of the planning council members, and the consensus is we accomplished a good deal at that gathering. Of course, it could have been better."

"That is the understatement of the year," I said. "I don't think anybody wants to be scared out of their wits thinking they might be shot."

"The reason I called," said George, changing the subject. "Our lake association holds an annual family gathering at Winter Lake County Park each summer, and we'd like to invite all the members of the planning council and their families to attend. I've talked to our members about it, and they would really like to meet the group."

"You sure?" I asked.

"I am. It's very informal. No speeches. Just a chance for our two groups to get to know each other a little better. It's potluck, so we ask everyone to bring something to share."

"George, thank you. I think it's a great idea."

"To be right up front with you, Scott, Jill Varsac and I were chatting at the Sunday picnic about how the lake owners could get their concerns about dropping water levels across to the planning council. And this would be one way of doing it. Just having people see the lake and meet the people with property here."

"Thank you, George. My goal all along is to get people talking with each other. I'm a firm believer that once people get to know each other, they usually can figure out a way of dealing with the problems they face."

"It's surely a step in the right direction," George said.

"I'll ask Gladys to send out the invitations to the planning council. What date did you set?"

"Labor Day, first Monday in September at eleven o'clock at Winter Lake County Park on the north end of the lake."

"We'll take care of the invitations," I said. "And again, thank you, George. The planning council is a little upset with what happened last Sunday. What you are planning sounds wonderful—a chance for them to get together with their families and get to know you folks and your families."

When I went to share with Gladys what George and I had discussed, Sarah had just arrived in the office.

"Good morning, Sarah," I said. "Nice morning."

"Good morning, Scott." She turned and headed for her office. I wondered what she was thinking, but she gave me no hint.

I discussed with Gladys what George's call was about, and she quickly got busy preparing invitations to go to the planning council members.

I returned to my office, thinking through how I should proceed with the planning council, especially since they will get George's invitation to meet with the lake owners in a couple of weeks. Gladys said she'd had calls from a few of the council members wondering if we were going to meet again or if the "farm-city picnic disaster," as one council member described it, meant that the council would likely disband.

I also had to consider the Ames County Fair was coming up in early September. At their July meeting, the fair board and its cadre of volunteers reported that all was in order for the fair. But now I wondered if I should ask the planning council to do something special at the fair.

The days flew by. I briefly met with Sarah as she explained what she, the 4-H leaders, and the Homemakers Organization members were planning for the upcoming Ames County Fair. She said, "The Homemakers are planning a big booth emphasizing the history of our Extension Office and how we have been of help to the citizens, both rural and urban, since way back in the mid-1900s. They haven't forgotten the petition that the Eagle Party had circulated asking people to sign that our office should be closed down. Frankly, the petition had one good side to it. It helped people realize that what you take for granted can disappear when you don't support it. Too many people thought the Extension Office would always be here. The petition got everybody's attention, that's for sure."

"Do you need any help with the booth?" I asked.

"I don't think so. Gladys found some old Extension bulletins and posters that we'll use tucked in the back of one of the closets. And several of the 4-H leaders and Homemaker members have everything, from 4-H member record books to copies of Homemaker recipes published over the years."

Sarah was all business. There was no hint of an invitation to wine, dinner, and more.

By week's end, Gladys had heard from every member of the planning council. They all planned to attend the event at Winter Lake County Park. She even heard from Jesse Johnson that he and his wife and daughter had planned to attend. I was sure that Johnson would be the one council member that some of the lake property owners were most angry with, as they firmly believed that he and his fellow large-acreage vegetable farmers were largely responsible for their lake nearly drying up. I also remembered that the Johnsons' daughter, Aimee, and the Hendersons' son, Josh, had been dating and that Jesse said something along the lines that no daughter of his would be dating a small-acreage pretend farmer. Sort of a tragic state of affairs, as I remembered what happened.

I asked Sarah if she planned to attend the event. She said she would be too busy working on preparations for the fair to attend.

37

Winter Lake Picnic

I drove out to Winter Lake County Park alone. I so wished Sarah had been with me. I wish I could get her out of my mind, but I just couldn't. I knew I should be thinking of what we had planned for the day. Who knew the planning council and the Winter Lake property owners would agree to meet? I know full well that some of the property owners, especially Mike Braun, hate my guts and believe I, along with the large commercial vegetable growers, are responsible for "his" lake drying up. I wonder if he'll be at the gathering. It'd be interesting to see what Mike and Jesse would have to say to each other. But I must say, just getting them standing next to each other would be a major achievement—at least in my way of thinking.

When I arrived at the park, I noticed a considerable crowd had already gathered. I forgot to ask Emerson how many people belonged to the Winter Lake Property Owners Association, but I guessed around thirty-five. I saw Lisa Lenfeld and Curtis Callahan, people I had met when I attended a meeting out here. George greeted me and introduced me to his wife.

"Do you think Mike Braun will be coming?" I asked, remembering too well the stunt at our office a few weeks ago when he arrived drunk, carrying a gun.

"I doubt it," said George. "In fact, I haven't seen him for a week or so. He heads up the local Eagle Party, as you know. I heard that three of their members who were protesting at the farm-city picnic were injured. One with a broken arm when somebody knocked him over in his hurry to run away from the firecracker explosions."

"I hadn't heard that," I said.

"You probably will. Word has it that the Eagle Party plans on suing your office for not providing a safe place for people attending the picnic."

"That's what I need—a lawsuit. One thing and another," I said, rubbing my head.

"I wouldn't worry about it," George said. "In fact, if they do bring suit against your office I'll volunteer my lawyer services—no charge."

"Thank you. Thank you so much."

I looked around and spotted council members busy chatting with lake owners and introducing their families to each other. I saw Aimee Johnson and Josh Henderson sitting at different tables but making eyes at each other. *I wonder if those two will get back together,* I thought.

I spotted Jill Varsac and Jodi Henderson standing by the lake, looking at the piers that were once in the water but were now high and dry. Looking at the tall grass growing where once there had been water. I wondered what they were talking about.

I also noticed that Jesse and his wife had walked down to the lake and quickly returned to the picnic area under the big, shady oak trees. I really wondered what they had said to each other.

Casseroles of every kind, baked beans and potato salad, three or four kinds of Jell-O, apple pie, blueberry pie, and strawberry pie covered two long picnic tables. I also saw a huge platter of sliced cheese and three or four kinds of cake. A platter was filled with steaming hamburgers and hot dogs that a couple of lake property owners grilled. A huge container of lemonade with chunks of ice in it stood at the end of one of the tables.

In a loud voice, George Emerson said, "First, let me welcome everyone here on this beautiful Labor Day afternoon. I'm so pleased that members of the recently organized Ames County Agricultural

Planning Council and their families have joined us today. Would the council members please stand?"

A nice round of applause erupted from the group. "Lake property owners, please introduce yourselves to these folks. I'm a member of the council, and they are a most interesting group. But enough talking. It's time to eat. And it looks like we won't go hungry today," George said as he pointed to the tables laden with food. *Finally, something is going well*, I thought. Nobody was protesting. Nobody was yelling at each other. Just a wonderful group of people enjoying food together in a park on a Sunday afternoon. *How I wished that Sarah could be here. That would have made the day perfect.*

I got in line with George and his wife. "Thank you, George," I said. "A great idea to bring these two groups together, and I couldn't think of a better way of doing it."

"You are most welcome." George filled his plate with the wonderful food spread out across the tables. I did the same, and sat down, relaxed, and decided to enjoy the afternoon.

I had just finished my meal when I heard a loud voice coming from behind me. I turned and saw someone walking toward the group. It was Mike Braun, and he was yelling. "What the hell is going on here? Tell me, what the hell is going on? This is our park. Who gave this bunch permission to use our park?"

Immediately, George was up and running toward Braun.

"What in the hell is going on here, George?" I heard Braun yell.

I couldn't hear what George was saying to a very red-faced Braun. I hadn't noticed before, but he was carrying a pistol. This time not in its holster, as had been the case when he came to our office.

George was holding up his arm, trying to calm down his neighbor, who was staggering just a little. I guessed he had been drinking.

"I see who's here. It's that damn planning council," he yelled. "Two people in that group I wanna see. Wanna kill the bastards. I see that damn Jesse Johnson sitting over there. I recognize him from his picture in the paper. Wanna put a bullet in him. He's the reason there is no water in our lake. His damn irrigation wells are the cause of it all. He and his damn farmer neighbors dried up our lake. I'm gonna solve the problem. Take the bastard out."

I glanced over at Johnson, and he was white as a sheet. His wife looked like she was about to pass out, and their daughter, Aimee, had begun to cry. The three of them seemed frozen in their seats.

"The second person I'm gonna shoot is that damn government county agent," Braun yelled as he pointed his pistol in my direction. "He's the son of a bitch that showed these damn farmers how to drain our lakes so they can water their freaking potatoes."

George said something to Braun that I could not hear.

Braun replied, "George, get the hell out of the way so you don't get hurt. I got no beef with you. It's that damn government worker and them big-shot potato farmers. Them's the guys I'm after."

Out of the corner of my eye I spotted Jodi, quietly and carefully moving around behind Braun. I knew he couldn't see her and wondered what she was doing. She better be careful, or she'd get hurt.

And then it happened. Jodi stood upright and began running full speed toward Braun. Before he had time to look around, she tackled him just below the knees, and he went crashing to the ground, his pistol flying out of his hand. She immediately jumped on him, with one knee placed firmly in the middle of his back.

I heard a collective gasp from the crowd as I saw Jodi sitting, pulling his hands behind his back.

"Anybody got a little piece of rope?" Jodi yelled. *What got into little mild-mannered yoga practicing Jodi*, I thought.

"Need a piece of rope," she repeated. I couldn't believe it. She was clearly in control of the situation while the rest of us sat petrified, wondering what would happen next. I can't remember when I was more scared. There is something about having someone point a gun at you and yell profanities that replaces any fearful memory I had before.

I noticed someone handing Jodi a shank of light rope, and she skillfully tied Braun's hands behind his back. Braun got to his feet and now saw who had tackled him.

"Son of a bitch," Braun said. "A damn woman got me. What's going on in this world? What in the hell is going on?" His face was red, and his words were slurred. I was now convinced that he had been drinking.

"Did anyone call 911 yet? We need the sheriff out here."

"I did," said George. "Dispatcher said a cruiser was on the way and will be here in a few minutes." Jodi picked up the pistol lying on the ground, checked to make sure it was loaded, and pointed it at Braun.

"You just stay put, and you'll be just fine," she said. I had never heard Jodi use this voice before and had known her for some time.

"You make one move, and you're gonna have a very sore leg," she said, pointing the pistol at a very distraught Braun.

I was dumbfounded at what I had just observed. Little Jodi Henderson took down a very angry Mike Braun and tied his hands like she had done this sort of thing every day. And how did she know so much about how to handle a pistol? It was then I remembered that she once told me she had spent a couple of years in the military. I didn't ask her what branch.

When I recovered my senses a bit, I walked over to Jodi and Braun, who sneered at me and said, "There'll be another day, government man. Another day."

"I don't think so," said Jodi. "You're a prime candidate for some time where there are bars on the windows."

"Jodi, thank you. Thank you." I said. I knew my hands were shaking. "I've just got to ask, where did you learn how to do this? I thought yoga was your thing."

Jodi smiled. "I spent a couple of years in the military police where you learn how to do this stuff."

Within fifteen minutes, a sheriff's deputy arrived and loaded a very confused and still quite drunk Mike Braun in the back of the cruiser for his trip to the county jail.

People lined up to shake Jodi's hand. First in line was a very shaken Jesse Johnson. "I ... I don't know how I can thank you," Johnson said. His voice was quivering. "You saved my life."

"Oh, I don't know about that. Drunks don't shoot very straight, and Mr. Braun was quite drunk."

It was Aimee Johnson who was next in line. "Thank you, thank you," she said. Tears were rolling down her face. "You saved my dad's life." She put her arms around Jodi and hugged her.

For the next several minutes people lined up to thank Jodi, who graciously took time to speak with each of them. In a loud voice, George finally broke in and said, "Well, I notice there is still some dessert on the table. I think I'll have some."

Several people joined him, but more decided to leave. I was wondering what was next. Two events in a row have come apart, each in its own way. The Ames County Planning Council was jinxed.

38
Office Discussion

When I arrived at the office on Tuesday morning, both Gladys and Sarah were waiting for me. I barely got through the door when both of them said, "What happened yesterday?" loud enough to rumble down the courthouse hall.

I tried to be cool about it all. "Oh, not much, really," I said. But I knew from the expressions on their faces that my "trying to be cool" ploy wasn't working.

"I heard the news on the Link Lake radio station this morning. Didn't catch it all, but the newscaster said there had been a near-shooting at the gathering you attended at Winter Lake. And some woman took out the would-be killer," Gladys said.

"That's about what happened," I said. "Would you believe that Jodi Henderson was once a military police officer? I did not know that. She was the woman who saved the day—saved my life likely."

"What'd Jodi do?" Sarah asked. She had the same concerned look on her face that he'd seen previously.

"Well, you both remember Mike Braun from the day he came in here with a pistol in his belt, yelling his fool's head off. He showed up at the picnic with another pistol, except this time it wasn't in his belt. He yelled that he wanted to kill two people that he saw at our gathering."

"Wanted to kill two people?" Gladys gasped.

"Yeah, that's what he said. He pointed his pistol at Jesse Johnson and scared the bejeebers out of him, his wife, and Aimee, his daughter. Braun blames Johnson and his irrigation system for draining his lake—he retired on Winter Lake a few years ago."

"Who was the second person?" Sarah asked.

"It was me," I tried to say without letting my emotions show, but I had difficulty doing it. I knew my hands were shaking, so I stuffed them into my pockets.

"It was you?" Sarah almost screamed. "Braun wanted to shoot you?"

"That's what he said. He was pointing his pistol at me when Jodi tackled him."

"Good God!" Sarah said. "Braun was planning to shoot you?"

"Afraid so. He says I taught the commercial vegetable growers how to irrigate their land, and this caused Winter Lake to dry up."

"Scott, this is just awful. What next? Threatening letters. Fake gunshots at our big farm-city picnic and then this," Sarah said as she left the room, holding her hands to her face.

I continued telling the story to Gladys. I tried to contain my emotions as I described what happened. I explained that this event might help bring some of the opposing factions together.

I said, "I know the entire group—both lake property owners and planning council members—now have something in common that both groups can talk about." I smiled, but my attempt at black humor hung in the air like a dirty cloud of cigar smoke.

"On a positive note," I said, "nearly every property owner apologized to members of the planning council for Braun's behavior. None of them see violence as a way of solving their disagreements. I am convinced of that, except for Mike Braun, of course. He's become enamored with the Eagle Party's fringe element's activities—a scary bunch."

Gladys picked up the phone that had just rung. "It's for you," she said, pointing to me.

"I'll take it in my office." I was happy not to have to say anything more about what clearly was the most upsetting thing I've ever encountered.

Sitting at my cluttered desk, I picked up the phone. "This is Scott Olson."

"It's Jesse Johnson."

"How are you doing?" I asked.

"To tell you the truth, I'm still shaking in my boots. I don't remember ever having anybody pointing a pistol at me and wanting to shoot me," Johnson said.

"Same for me. My hands are still shaking."

"Guess we've gotta move on. That's what my wife tells me anyway. Got a couple of things on my mind," Johnson said.

"How can I help?"

"First, this Jodi Henderson. I must confess I haven't gotten to know her very well. I guess it's pretty obvious that some of my fellow vegetable growers who raise several hundreds of acres of vegetables and I have kind of looked down on those small-acreage farmers like Jodi. But she is really something. I mean really something. Here she's a farmer and obviously knows how to get her hands dirty. But what she did yesterday. Well, it's amazing. Here we all sit, scared to death and not having a clue what to do, and Jodi takes charge of the situation. That Braun guy is really unhinged. One time I thought the Eagle Party was on to something—but if he's the head of it, I don't want a thing to do with it. Anyway, one of my reasons for calling is about Jodi. I'd like to nominate her for some kind of hero award. I think she saved a bunch of lives yesterday, mine included. And she made it look easy, like something she might do every day."

"She surely surprised me as well. I did not know she had been in the military police," I said.

"Anyway," continued Johnson, "who do I contact to nominate her for an award? She surely deserves it. My wife reminded me that I could be dead today. And she's right. Braun was there to do me in, and he doesn't care for you either, Scott."

"Oh, you noticed." I chuckled. I'm sure this was the first time I'd broken a smile in two days. "Contact the county's sheriff's office here in Willow River. The sheriff will help you with the award for Jodi." I checked my Rolodex—yes, I still have one—for the sheriff's phone number and gave it to him.

"The second thing I want to talk to you about, Scott, is Winter Lake."

"Yes," I said, wondering where this was going.

"You know, when I was a kid, my dad and I fished that lake. It was one really good fishing lake. One of the best in this part of Ames County," Johnson said.

"It was like that ten years ago when I first moved here. I'd fished it a couple of times then, too," I said.

"I've been darn busy the last half dozen years, trying to make my vegetable growing business work. I've made some good money with my peas, sweet corn, and potatoes. So have my neighbors. I'd heard talk that the water levels for Winter Lake and some of the other lakes in the area had been dropping the last few years. I thought it was just one of the regular cycles. Several years the water is up, and several years it's down. You know about that, of course."

"Yes, I do," I said, now wondering what Johnson had on his mind.

"I read in the paper about the lake levels being low. Now I hate to admit this, but I had no idea that Winter Lake is only about half the size it was ten years ago. Scott, be honest with me now. Do you think our high-capacity irrigation pumps had something to do with what's happened to Winter Lake?"

"Yes, yes, I do believe that." I wondered if Johnson would hang up on me. But he didn't.

"There's research to back that up?" Johnson asked.

"Yes, there is. A bunch of it, coming right out of the university in Stevens Point."

"How do I get a hold of some of those research reports? I'd like to read them."

"I'll make some copies and send the reports to you," I said.

"Very much appreciated," said Johnson. "Thank you, and we'll be in touch. Oh, by the way, when is the next meeting of the planning council?"

"Soon. We haven't set the date yet."

Well, I'll be, I thought as I hung up the phone. *Maybe some good will come out of all of this yet.* I don't know why I remembered this, but I remember an old-timer from Missouri once telling me how difficult it was to teach a mule anything. He said, "The first thing you've got to do is get the mule's attention."

"And how do you do that?" I remember asking.

"You hit the mule over the head with a two-by-four."

No question about it. Having a gun pointed at him surely got Jesse's attention. Now we'll see what kind of learning results. Many years ago, I also remember one of my university professors saying, "There is a lot more to teaching than telling." I remember how he discussed what he called a "learning environment." By that, he meant trying to provide situations where people can learn about something without realizing that they are learning it. I've been trying to do that by bringing these various groups of people together, getting acquainted with each other, and learning from each other. But with all the turmoil that has resulted, I'd begun to question my strategy. But now, with Jesse's phone call, I felt a glimmer of success. True, I didn't want a crazy person threatening to shoot people, like what happened at Winter Lake. But some good may have come of it.

Moments later, there was a gentle knock on my door, and Sarah entered and closed it behind her.

"Scott, I'm so sorry." I could see that she was trying to hold back tears, but she wasn't succeeding. "Are you okay?"

"About as good as expected, considering I was about to be shot."

"It's awful, Scott. Just awful." She began crying.

I handed her a tissue from the box I kept in the lower drawer of my desk.

"I ... I," she said between sobs. "Would you, would you stop by my cabin tonight?"

39
Scott and Sarah

The day flew by. I even found time to complete some reports I knew were a couple of weeks late. I wondered if my district director, Ben Ruskie, would accept having a guy pointing a gun at me as an excuse for being a little late with my reports. I guessed that he wouldn't. For Ruskie, there was no excuse for being late with a report. I don't know how many times he had reminded me of that.

I also noticed that I had a backlog of emails—they could wait for another day. I stopped at my apartment before heading out to Sarah's place. I shaved, showered, and put on some fresh clothes—trying to remove the smell of fear, which I knew was all over me.

I wondered whether Sarah merely wanted to talk. In our relationship she had always been the talker. I was more reticent. I usually kept things to myself—she couldn't understand that. She worked hard at pulling my feelings out of me. Sometimes she succeeded. But mostly not. It frustrated her. Her frustration had reached a boiling point a few weeks ago when she yelled at me. She had never yelled at me before. And then I left, closed the door when I could have stayed and talked and shared more of what she wanted to hear. I should have told her how much I loved her. But I didn't do that. How I wished that I had because the last several days had been agony, believing that our relationship had ended. Ten-plus years down the drain. What a fool

I was. But do I have the guts to tell her that?

I parked my truck in the secret place I had always parked, walked up to the cabin door, and knocked, not knowing what to expect. I caught the wonderful smell of Sarah's cooking. I wondered what she had prepared for supper.

Sarah opened the door and stood there for a moment. How beautiful she was. Her blue eyes sparkled. Her smile was as wide as I'd ever seen it.

"Hi," I said, not knowing what else to say. Before I could consider any more words, she pulled me into the room and shut the door.

"Hi, yourself," she said as she wrapped her arms around me, kissed me, and then led me toward her bedroom.

Sometime later, the two of us sat at her table, enjoying a glass of wine and chatting—mostly about nothing. It was like it had always been when we were together. Two people who loved each other enjoying each other's company. Soon we were enjoying supper, a little overcooked, as dinner was a bit later than usual.

"I'm sorry I walked out on you," I blurted out. "I knew you wanted to talk. I don't know what I was thinking." I took both of her hands in mine when I said it. I saw tears in her eyes.

"Can we both forget that night?" Sarah said with a bit of a smile. "The last few days have been awful, and not just because of what has been happening at work."

"Agreed."

Changing the subject, Sarah asked, "Have you looked at your emails for the last couple of days?"

"I have not," I confessed. "I guess I just didn't want to wade through all the junk mail I get every day and then find a serious email with somebody ticked off about something I recently said or did."

"You get some of those?" Sarah asked, now smiling broadly.

"I suspect you don't."

"You're kidding, of course," Sarah said. "I just got one yesterday from one of those Eagle Party people who chewed me out for working with single mothers in the county, trying to help them with their budgeting, meal planning, that sort of thing."

"What did it say?"

"Well this guy—I assumed it was a guy—went off on a rant about how if these single mothers had stayed married, or not gotten married in the first place, they wouldn't have all of these problems. And that the government shouldn't be wasting hardworking taxpayer money trying to help them out. He ended with the old cliché: 'She made her bed, now she should sleep in it.'"

"It figures," I said. "I get a couple of emails every day from an Eagle Party member with the same tone—get the government out of the lives of people. At least Mike Braun won't be bothering us for a while. He's likely due for some prison time."

"I'll bet Braun is the guy behind those threatening letters, maybe even behind getting the kid to set off the firecrackers at the picnic," Sarah said.

"I hope so. I don't know how much longer I could put up with all of that nonsense," I said.

"Hardly nonsense," Sarah said. "Not when people's lives are at stake."

We both sat quietly for a bit, looking out over the quiet waters of Ames Lake. I spotted a couple of boats with fishermen, but the lake was quiet otherwise.

"There was one email that troubled me a little bit, beyond the usual stuff I get every day," said Sarah.

"And that would be?"

"Well, it was from our boss, Ben Ruskie, the word mangler and Internet genius," said Sarah.

"What did he have to say?"

"He started out writing about how much he appreciated all the hard work each of us county people was doing. But then he began talking about the Eagle Party. He wrote that they had some serious questions about Extension and what it was doing these days," she said.

"He just figured out that the Eagle Party is not one of our fans," I said.

"Apparently so. He went on to say that the legislature was in the midst of developing its next budget and that he would keep us informed of their decisions," Sarah said.

"So what do you think he is trying to tell us?"

"From my point of view, he's not saying anything that we don't already know. But there might be more. Who knows?" Sarah said.

40
Fred and Oscar

Ames County Gazette

Editorial

As many of you know, under the capable leadership of Scott Olson, County agricultural agent for Ames County, an Ames County Agricultural Planning Council has been meeting and sponsoring various events in the county. As editor of this newspaper, I have been privileged to be a member of that council.

The council's purpose is to help the people of Ames County, those who live in the cities and villages, as well as those living in the country and around our beautiful lakes. To better understand each other and, when needed, help each other.

There has been festering disagreement within the agricultural sector itself. The county boasts a number of large commercial farmers including several dairy farmers in the county that milk more than one thousand cows. Ames County also has a growing number of large-acreage vegetable growers who depend on irrigation to grow their crops. Perhaps the fastest growing element in our agricultural sector is the small-acreage farmers, mainly growing vegetables that they sell directly to schools, restaurants, and at farmers' markets. In recent years, these two farmer groups have not always seen eye to eye.

A growing concern in recent years has pitted the lake property owners against the large commercial farmers, especially those who irrigate their crops. The lake property owners blame the farmers for drying up their lakes.

To add to the unhappy mix of characters in Ames County, an environmental group, Citizens for the Future, has voiced their concerns about soil erosion and especially about the overuse of water by the irrigation farmers, as water pollution caused by the large dairy operations in the county.

Agricultural planning council events have tried to bring these various factions together—indeed, representatives of each group serve on the council. Slowly, they have begun to know each other and, I hope, appreciate each other a little more.

But alas, with the exception of the dairy breakfast, which came off without a hitch and brought several hundred people in touch with a working dairy farm, there have been problems, including one near catastrophe.

I don't know if our readers are aware that our county agent has received threatening hate mail as a result of trying to bring these sometimes warring factions together. As a result, the local police have been on high alert and may have overreacted at a planning council farm-city event, where some kid set off firecrackers, resulting in a stampede of people leaving the event.

But what happened at Winter Lake stands out as an event that could have had a tragic result. I, as a member of the planning council, along with my wife, attended the event, and I must confess I was scared out of my wits when one of the lake owners, who had been drinking and was known to have violent tendencies, arrived carrying a loaded pistol. He threatened to kill one of the vegetable farmers who he accused of drying up "his" lake, and he also threatened to shoot Scott Olson.

Had it not been for Jodi Henderson, a small-acreage farmer representative on our planning council and a former army military police officer, there may have been some shooting deaths. Henderson succeeded in overpowering the angry lake owner, tying him up and holding him until a sheriff's deputy arrived and arrested him.

I sincerely hope we all have learned something from these events, especially the one at Winter Lake. Violence does not solve problems; it only creates more. As difficult as it may seem at the time, we must get to know those with views different from ours. And then have a civil discussion about out disagreements.

Sometimes I think we have forgotten how to discuss our differences, but we must do so with factual information. That's where Scott Olson and the Extension Office serve a vital role in our community. His office has direct access to the research findings of Badger State University.

These days, with social media, talk radio, and TV commentators spewing opinions rather than facts, we all have a considerable responsibility to sort through all that we hear and see, and then, with careful thinking, and only then do we share with others our take on a given issue.

We must move forward. We must give the Ames County Agricultural Planning Council an opportunity to help us solve our differences.

"You read the editorial in this week's *Gazette*?" Oscar asked Fred as they sat across from each other, enjoying an early morning cup of coffee at the Black Oak Café.

"Yup, I did," answered Fred as he took a big sip of coffee, no sugar, no cream.

"So, Fred. What's your take on it?"

"What do you mean 'what's my take'? Where'd you come up with language like that? You been doin' too much book readin'.

"What'd you get out of it? What'd you learn from what the editor had to say?"

"Well," Fred hesitated for a moment. "Got one big thing from readin' that piece."

"And that would be?" asked Oscar.

"There are people out there with guns, and they intend to use them, and they want to shoot people we know. That's the big thing I learned. And, by golly, it scares the hell out of me. It really does. To think somebody would try to shoot somebody else right in front of their family at a picnic. Well, that's just awful. What in hell has gone wrong with this country? Tell me that."

"You got yourself a point there, Fred. You got a point."

"I know what I'm gonna do. Didn't take much thinking to figure it out, either. Didn't need to do any research."

"What are you gonna do, Fred?"

"This is what I'm gonna do. In fact, I already started doin' it." Fred picked up his coffee and took a long drink. He looked around the room to see if anyone appeared to be listening in on their conversation.

"When I go to bed at night, I've got right next to me my loaded double-barrel 12-gauge shotgun," Fred said in a near whisper.

"You what?"

"You heard me, Oscar. Anybody try to shoot me is gonna wish he didn't try," said Fred.

"Good God, Fred. You'll end up shootin' your cat."

"I ain't got no cat."

"You should have a cat, Fred. Every farmer should have a cat."

"But you just said that if I had a cat, I'd end up shootin' it because I would think it was one of them gun-totin' guys like the fella at Winter Lake."

"Forget what I said, Fred. It was just a manner of speaking. That if you slept with your shotgun you'd end up shootin' something you didn't intend to shoot. You ever think you might shoot yourself in the foot?"

Both men were quiet for a few moments, enjoying their coffee and the smells of bacon frying and sweet rolls coming out of the oven.

"Well, you do what you want, Fred. But I'm not about to go to bed with a shotgun."

"Suit yourself, Oscar. But if one of those crazies with a gun shows up in our neighborhood, I'm wondering which of us will be sitting at this table by himself. I'm wondering about that."

41
County Fair Planning

I mostly felt good about coming to work after Sarah and I patched up our relationship, which I thought might be doomed. It surely wasn't. She seemed even more distraught than I was after I walked out on her the night she lost her temper with me.

The Ames County Fair was coming up fast, and after hearing from several of the planning council members that we should meet and discuss various activities the council could sponsor, I set a meeting. Frankly, I was a bit taken aback by several council members' interest in meeting. Given all of the problems and challenges at the various council functions, I wouldn't have been surprised if the council had decided to dissolve. Of course, the altercation at Winter Lake was the worst. I thought after that, nobody would want anything to do with the planning council, but just the opposite happened.

The Winter Lake near-shooting brought council members together better than anything I could have planned. It's a shame that it works that way, but I can remember when I was a kid and one of our neighbor's barns caught fire, and the entire neighborhood came to help him save his cattle and much of his farm equipment. The neighborhood was different after that.

With the planning council coming together, I hoped we could move further in bringing some of the county's feuding factions together.

I called the meeting for ten o'clock in the morning and wondered what kind of agenda I should put together. I'd asked someone on the council to chair previous meetings, but I decided to do this one myself. Maybe I shouldn't have an agenda and just let the meeting flow. I knew this strategy would fly in the face of what my boss, Ben Ruskie, and other administrators advocated with the tired phrase: Plan your work, work your plan. Sometimes, I discovered that not having a plan may be the plan. Ruskie would never understand that.

There was a knock on the door. I glanced at the clock; it read 9:30. Gladys came in. "Jeff Miles from the bank is here and wondered if he could talk with you.

He came early for the ten o'clock meeting."

"Sure. Send him in." I wondered what he wanted. He had attended all of the council's meetings but usually had little to say. I wondered if it might be about Sarah.

Jeff entered, and I gestured for him to sit down. "Jeff, how are you? Recovered from the fiasco out at Winter Lake?"

"Not really. Hard to get over something like that. What about you, Scott? He was pointing his gun right at you."

"Well, to be honest, Jeff, I was never more scared in my life."

"Don't blame you. Just an awful situation. Downright awful."

"So what can I do for you?"

"I want to apologize for not volunteering to do more in helping with the planning council's various activities. That planning council is a great idea. I must confess, I wasn't so sure it would work, and it was just another committee with a new name that met and met and didn't do anything."

"Thanks. No need to apologize for not doing more with the council. You were busy with a new job," I said. "By the way, your idea of asking old-timers to write something about early days on the farm worked out well, as you probably noticed."

"I read the articles in the paper. Most interesting, and you know, what these folks wrote about was just about the same that the folks in Dunn County wrote about when we did this there."

"Thanks again for the idea."

"Our bank plans to have a booth at the fair, as you probably know. But if you need help with anything else, let me know. I promised Jill Varsac that I'd help her in her booth as well—she and her group are doing some interesting things," Jeff said.

"Her work is not always appreciated," I said.

"How well I know," Jeff said. "But the more I talk with her, the more I believe she and her group have a lot to say—especially as we look to the future of agriculture and its relationship to the environment."

"I couldn't agree more." I glanced at my watch. "Best we move across the hall to the meeting. I hear voices in the outer office. I've got to gather up a few things, and I'll see you in a couple minutes."

I walked across the hall to the meeting room and saw the entire group—except Jodi—seated around the table, chatting with each other as if they were old friends. I wondered if she was sick or hadn't planned to come. I'd no more than had the thought when she appeared at the door with a big smile on her face.

Immediately, everyone in the room stood up and began clapping. An embarrassed and red-faced Jodi stood quietly, looking down as she received the most heartfelt thanks I'd ever seen. The clapping continued.

"Enough already," Jodi said, holding up her hand. "I understand this group has work to do."

"Jodi," I began, my voice breaking with emotion, "I know you've heard this before, but thank you. Thank you. Thank you. You saved my life." The clapping began again, this time louder than before.

When the clapping subsided, I tried to bring my emotions under control and mostly succeeded. I quickly discovered that the group was more interested in Jodi's background than anything else.

"I didn't know you were in the military police," Emil said. "How come you never told us that?"

"Nobody asked," Jodi said. "Besides, it really isn't something I like to talk about. I'd rather talk about how to grow carrots and lettuce."

Her last comments evoked a few smiles.

"Weren't you scared out of your wits? I mean, that guy had a loaded gun, and he could have shot you just like that," said Jill.

"Sure, I was scared, but I also have been trained to deal with situations like that," Jodi said, trying not to sound boastful.

"You know you've been nominated for a State Hero Award," said Harvey.

"I heard that, but I'm no hero. I was just doing what needed to be done."

Eventually, after a few more minutes of questions and answers, the council, now a closely knit working group, began discussing what things they might do at the Ames County Fair to help achieve some of the council's goals. Soon I was writing on the board:

"Planning council booth"
"Extension Office booth"
"4-H speaking contest focusing on water and its importance"
"Parade of old tractors"
"Farmers' market featuring small-acreage farmers' products"

As the meeting ended, I thought, *Wow, without an agenda, without much of a plan, this group is on its way.* But my practical, realistic side had to think of what happened at our recent sponsored events. I decided to call Chief Wilkins to share some of my fears.

"This is Scott Olson," I said. "The fair is coming up in a couple weeks."

"Scott, I know what you're gonna say, and I'm way ahead of you. We're gonna have twice as much manpower at the fair than we usually do. We'll do everything we can to make sure there are no incidents."

"Thank you," I said. "The Eagle Party and their anti-government group is still out there. You remember that Mike Braun was head of that bunch."

"How could I forget?" said the chief.

42
Unexpected Email

Planning for the annual Ames County Fair hummed along like I'd never seen before. No grumbling. People volunteered. The usual problems, including the leaky roof on the 4-H food building that needed fixing and replacing one of the sick cattle judges, all seemed like minor annoyances after all I had faced. I suspect I'd handled these sorts of problems in other years and had elevated them to levels of importance that they did not deserve.

Sarah also seemed her happy self as we worked together, always with the hope that this year's county fair would be bigger and better than ever. Of course, we had that hope every year.

The weather forecast for this year's fair was clear and sunny for Thursday and Saturday, with a possible shower on Friday night and rain again on Sunday, the last day of the fair. I'd hoped for a better forecast. I remember that last year it rained two of the four days of the fair, cutting our attendance by about a third.

The days running up to the fair were mostly a blur, though pleasant, as I always liked county fairs. The Ames County Fair was one of the better ones in central Wisconsin, thanks to the vast network of volunteers who did everything from helping sell food in the 4-H food tent to helping each of the various judges. You name it—cattle, vegetables, canned fruits, fine arts, photography, rabbits, sheep, goats, geese, ducks—and it showed up at the Ames County Fair to be judged and have ribbons placed on the winners.

Thursday was entry day, meaning men, women, and children hauled their entries to the fairgrounds. The 4-H boys and girls led their prize calves into the cattle barn, shuffled their hogs into the hog barn, and found a home for their poultry projects and their woodworking entries. Wonderful pandemonium. Little kids and big kids, calm parents and excited parents, all worked together and enjoyed every minute of it, for the county fair was the highlight of the year for 4-H members and nearly everyone in the county, whether they were involved in agriculture or not.

Representatives of the various organizations in the county, the Republican Party, the Democratic Party, the Eagle Party, the Ames County Historical Society, the Vegetable Growers Association, and the small-acreage farmers were busy putting up their booths and displays. I spotted Jeff Miles helping Jill Varsac and several other members of the CFTF group put up their booth—like the one at the farm-city picnic, which featured water. I had a passing thought. *Is something going on between Jeff and Jill? A banker and an environmentalist?*

With the help of several members of the County Homemakers Organization and the county 4-H leaders, Sarah put up a booth depicting past and present Extension Office activities in the county. I spent an hour or so helping them.

The various churches in the county had booths. I saw the Lutherans, the Methodists, and the Presbyterians working on their booths. There were likely others as well.

Implement dealers from throughout the county brought in everything from mammoth diesel tractors that the large-acreage farmers commonly used to much smaller tractors, their size reminiscent of when I was a kid.

In the commercial building, I saw displays of everything from "Liniment that helps cure almost everything" to "How to cook when you don't have much to cook."

That evening, when everything had found its place and quiet settled over the fairgrounds, save for the occasional bellow of a cow or a turkey intent on gobbling every few minutes, I decided to stop by my office to see if I had any last-minute emails or phone calls that needed attending.

I scrolled through the long list of emails—sometimes topping fifty or seventy-five a day—and stopped on one from my boss, Ben Ruskie. I immediately thought I must have been late with one of my reports; that's about the only time I heard anything from Ruskie. Thankfully, he mostly left our little Extension staff in Ames County alone. I'd heard from some of my colleagues in larger counties that he stopped by every couple of weeks with some harebrained idea he wanted them to try.

I clicked on the email and read:

To all County Extension Staff:

You are all aware that the state of Wisconsin continues to face serious budget problems: Roads and bridges need repair, state parks lack funding, the DNR has insufficient funds to carry out its various mandates, military veteran care requires a budget increase, and more.

You are likely also aware that our current administration has been working hard to lower taxes for Wisconsin's citizens. As our governor has recently said, "We've got to make some serious cuts, and we must all learn how to do more with less."

Those cuts are in the next state legislative budget, and the governor has said he will sign it. Extension's state administrators have seen this coming but had not anticipated that the budget cuts would be so deep and would affect our Extension operations so much.

Below is the decision that the state Extension director and his staff have made in consultation with the district directors:

Every county Extension staff in Wisconsin must cut its professional staff by one person. I'm sorry to bring you this bad news. And I know that the county Extension staffs, working with their audiences, will make the right decision about which staff member to cut.

I want you to know that we in administration are working hard to develop new models for bringing valuable research information from Badger State University to the people of the great state of Wisconsin. Thankfully, we have social media to help us do that. We are also examining creative staffing models that, in some instances, will involve county Extension staff serving more than one county.

Please contact me if you have any questions.

Sincerely,
Ben Ruskie, District Director

I read the email a second time. In true Ruskie form, he waited until the end of the email to say what he wanted to say. I sat back in my chair and ran my fingers through my hair. I could feel a terrific headache building in the back of my neck.

Why do I have to get such awful information during the fair, which comes close to being the highlight of my year? I wondered if Sarah had seen this. She would have gotten the same email. *Should I call her and tell her in case she hasn't read it? Or wait until tomorrow?*

And the bigger question: Which of us should leave? Sarah? Me? How do we decide?

43

Ames County Fair

Sarah answered on the second ring.

"Hi, Scott. What's up? Somebody got a problem at the fair? Seemed to be humming right along when I left for home."

"Fair is doing well," I said. "I just got around to reading my emails. Got one from Ben Ruskie that's more than a little upsetting."

"I saw it," Sarah said. "Just awful, that's what it is. Couldn't have come at a worse time. You want to stop by the cabin?"

"I really don't want to talk about it. Not tonight anyway."

"Who said anything about talking?" I could hear the sweet smile in her voice.

Before leaving for the fairgrounds, I checked the weather forecast once more: Possibility of thunderstorms late Friday evening, ending by early morning. Clear on Saturday. Heavy rain predicted for Sunday. Weather was always a concern at the fair. And weather people were often wrong. I was hoping that what was predicted for Sunday could hold off until Monday.

Friday was judging day at the fair, and the 4-H members who had entered their various projects got to see how their work stacked up with their fellow 4-H'ers. It was an exciting time for each 4-H member. Their volunteer leaders and parents stood by watching as the various judges examined the 4-H'ers' work, whether it was a dairy calf, a lamb, a rabbit, a woodworking project, or a box of freshly picked vegetables. It was also an exciting day for me as I moved from one judging area to another to see if all was going well, and it was.

I tried to keep a professional, optimistic, and happy face, but it was tough knowing that either Sarah or I would be losing our jobs by the end of the year. I tried to keep my mind off how we would make that decision. I knew the procedure. The Ames County administrator would likely have received an email similar to mine. She would send it to Bill Workman, the longtime chair of the county board's Extension Education Committee. He and his committee would discuss it. And knowing Bill, he would first talk with Sarah and me about it. But the decision in Madison had been made. Bottom line, no matter who discussed it and how much discussion took place, one of us would lose our jobs. The more I thought about it, the more angry I became. I should be thinking about the fair. Maybe I'm too into what the Ames County Agricultural Planning Council is doing. We surely have had our ups and down, but in my humble judgment, the council's work is beginning to pay off. People who would never talk to each other are now talking. It's an important beginning.

I walked by the booth sponsored by the Ames County Commercial Vegetable Growers, who depend on irrigation for their crops. I looked for Jesse Johnson, the group's president, but I didn't see him.

"Is Jesse here?" I asked. Several vegetable growers I recognized were in the booth.

"No he's not," said a member of the group that I don't remember meeting.

"Will he be back soon?"

"I don't think so," the fellow said. "He's no longer president of our group, you know."

"Really?" is all I could think to say.

"Yup. We voted him out last week. Not the leader we need these days," the fellow said.

I decided not to follow up, but I quickly surmised that Johnson had shared some of the research findings I had sent him, and they didn't go down well with the group that wanted to deny that irrigation could have any serious effect on drawing down the aquifer or causing lake levels in their community to drop. *So much for progress with this group*, I thought.

I glanced at my watch. It was nearly ten, the time when the 4-H speaking contest was to begin. I hurried over to the 4-H building, where a little stage had been erected with a podium. I noticed about fifty folding chairs lined up in front of the stage, all filled. I saw Josh Henderson, Jodi's son, and Aimee Johnson, Jesse's daughter, sitting toward the back, holding hands. I remembered when Aimee had stopped by the office, crying and sharing that her father had told her she must no longer date Josh. I thought, *Looks like the planning council had some results beyond those intended.* Standing behind the podium was a 4-H'er who looked to be about twelve years old. She had some papers in front of her, but her speaking coach had obviously taught her not to read her speech.

"Thank you all for coming," she said confidently. "Are you all able to hear me okay?" I noticed people nodding that they could hear just fine.

"I'm talking about water today—something we all take for granted. We need water to live. Did you know that we can go a few weeks without eating and still live, but unless we have water about every one hundred hours, we will die? That's true of everything that lives— plants, animals, trees.

"Do we worry about using too much water? Well, we should. Because as our population increases, we will need more water. Water to raise our crops. Water to feed our animals. And water for us to drink and brush our teeth and shower."

The more I listened to this young woman, who talked with a clear, confident voice, the more impressed I was. I wished her audience of fifty, mostly parents and fellow 4-H'ers, would have been an audience of five thousand. Her message is one everyone should hear, and hear often.

When she finished her half-hour talk, everyone clapped loudly. I'm sure her parents were proud of her; I surely was. I've seen this happen time and time again: a young, shy person enrolls in 4-H, is encouraged to learn about speaking in public, and in a few years, becomes a first-rate speaker with no stumbling and mumbling. They can stand tall, eloquently relaying what they have to say. I am constantly annoyed and, unfortunately, see evidence almost every day of speakers mumbling along, hoping to think of something to say, whether speaking to a group live, on the radio, or TV—words without meaning. Even worse is when people do not consider their words before speaking or lack evidence of facts to support what they say.

As I think about what's going through my mind and contemplate one more cut in our office staff, I think about what will happen to the 4-H program that has done such a wonderful job with out-of-school educational programming in preparing our county's young people for a mostly unknown future.

I was walking along the midway, past the Ferris wheel, the Tilt-A-Whirl, and the merry-go-round, past the milk bottles game and the 4-H food building that was doing a brisk business selling hamburgers, chocolate milk, and ice cream cones. I ordered a hamburger and chocolate milk and sat down at a picnic table to enjoy a quick lunch. I noticed a young woman walking up to me. She looked familiar, but I couldn't place her.

"Ann Arnold, from the police department," she said. "How're you doing since the altercation out at Winter Lake?"

"Well, to be honest, some days are better than others." Now I know why I didn't recognize Ann when I first saw her. She wore a uniform that day I met her in the restaurant. Today she was in plain clothes, as were several other police officers working the fairgrounds, hoping to stop any trouble before it started.

"Got some good news from the crime lab in Madison this morning. Thought I might see you here to tell you."

I wondered what good news she had, but any good news would be welcome, considering my life the last few days.

"Fellow at the lab said that they have nearly figured out the puzzle of the threatening letters," she said. "They're doing a little follow-up to make sure they're right before giving us an answer."

I had put the two threatening letters out of my mind, especially since Mike Braun was jailed. He hadn't admitted it, but I was sure he was the culprit. I looked forward to the crime lab confirming what I knew was true.

"Well, that is good news. Thanks for telling me." I went on to tell Ann that I was almost positive that Mike Braun had done it.

"You'll be the first to know when I hear from the lab."

"Thanks," I said. "Thank you very much." Several months ago, way back in April, a rock with the first letter crashed through the window at the community center. Frankly, I didn't really expect an answer from the crime lab. I'm sure they had more important things to do than figure out who wrote a couple of letters.

I stopped by the entertainment tent, which featured local musicians from eleven in the morning until four in the afternoon. The tent seated about a hundred or so people, and every chair was filled as local accordion player Johnnie Jay played and sang the songs that old-timers in Ames County liked: polkas, waltzes, and sing-alongs.

I couldn't help but wonder what would happen to the Ames County Fair with only one Extension agent in the Ames County office. Sarah and I spent more hours working on the fair than anyone ever imagined. From the early planning stages to supervising the hundred or so volunteers that made the fair work, to arranging for the performers for the entertainment, and much more.

I continued doing what I liked best at the county fair—talking with farmers, implement dealers, and 4-H members, their parents and leaders. I talked with people who stopped by the Extension booth, where I spent most of my time. I answered questions about what we do and have done in the past. I answered questions about the Eagle Party's petition to close down the Extension Office because it was just one more unneeded government program. I didn't have the heart to tell these people that the state Eagle Party has nearly succeeded in closing down our office as there will be just one Extension agent plus Gladys, our long-suffering secretary, left in the office at year's end.

44

Paul Workman

At quarter of ten, I wanted to stop by the Extension booth where Sarah was still working. The fair would close down at ten for the evening, and I wanted to offer to help her put the booth to bed for the night. As I approached, I heard a loud man's voice, nearly shouting, and thought I remembered the voice. It was Paul Workman, Bill's son. How could I forget the voice? I remember how he yelled at me a few months ago when he and his dad stopped by my office.

"I must tell you, young lady, that this county doesn't need any more of your damn meddling. You've stirred up a whole bunch of women. Stirred them up so bad that they refused to sign the petition we tried to circulate throughout the county trying to close down this useless office."

No one else was around, only Paul and a very tired Sarah, who was taking this all in without saying a word. I knew she probably remembered Paul's tirade in the office and thought he was one of those behind drafting the petition to close down their office. But I guessed she didn't know that since Mike had been jailed, Paul had been elected president of the Ames County Eagle Party.

Paul's rant continued as I hurried toward the Extension booth. "A woman's place is in the home, taking care of her husband, taking care of the kids, cooking, baking, sewing. We sure as hell don't need any more women like that damn Jodi Henderson who took down Mike. Dirty shame that happened. A dirty damn shame. Mike's a good man. He knows what's right. Now he sits in jail when the party has so much work to do."

I wondered if Paul had a gun. I hadn't asked Chief Wilkins if they checked people coming into the fair to make sure none carried weapons. Eagle Party members hated that and argued that they should have the right to carry a gun everywhere, whether it was in church, in school, or at the county fair.

"What's going on here?" I said, trying to sound unafraid and confident.

"Oh, I see you're still around. Thought you'd be home by now, with your feet up."

"What's all this yelling about?" I asked.

"Well, I'm trying to make this colleague of yours understand that her meddling in the lives of the county's women is unacceptable."

"So, you think her work as a representative of Badger State University is meddling?" I asked with what I hoped was a confident voice.

"You're damn right it is. Women's place is in the home. That's where this woman ought to be." He pointed a long finger at Sarah. "She ought to be home, married to some guy and takin' care of his kids. Here she sits, trying to be a big shot," said Paul in a voice too loud.

"You think so, huh?" I said, moving right in front of him. "You really think so?"

"You're damn right I do, and I got a bunch of people agreeing with me. If you haven't noticed," he said in the most sneering voice I'd ever heard.

"Well, you don't get your point across by shouting at my colleague," I said. I was tired from a long day, my head had begun to hurt, and I found myself doing what I tried to avoid doing—arguing with someone who believed he was right, with no hope of changing his mind.

"Well, hell, this Sarah is part of the problem. And by the way, the sooner we shut down this damn Extension Office, the better this county's gonna be. You do your share of meddling, too, if you don't think we've noticed. You sure have done a number on my dad. Poor damn fool thinks the world of you."

I smiled at his last comment. Bill had been a friend and supporter from the first day I stepped foot in Ames County. I wondered what Bill would think if he knew his red-faced, agitated son was intent on disparaging the work that Sarah and I have been doing over the years.

"I think you'd better go on home, Paul," I said. "Fairgrounds close at ten tonight."

"You ain't heard the last of me." He turned on his heel and walked away.

"Well, that was something," I said, looking at a clearly upset Sarah, who had endured Paul's tirade for the past several minutes.

"Guess I didn't know how much those Eagle Party guys hated women, especially women who did things those guys think they shouldn't be doing."

"I don't know what's up with these guys. They're kind of a throwback to the turn of the century. But even then, I don't think men treated women like these guys do."

"He didn't give me a chance to say anything," Sarah said, running a hand through her hair.

"You're a real trooper, Sarah. You don't deserve to have someone talk to you like that."

"I'm heading home, Scott. I'm absolutely beat. I'll see you tomorrow."

I headed for my car parked on the far end of the fairgrounds. As I walked, I thought about everything that had happened that day. Even knowing that our office staff would soon be cut in half, I rather enjoyed the day—until this debacle with Paul. I wondered if I should talk to his dad about what happened tonight. I'll have to think some more about that. Bill would be devastated to hear what his son had done that evening.

I didn't hear the footsteps behind me until they were too close. I turned to look and saw a tall figure moving toward me. I couldn't identify who it was before I saw a hand come up holding what appeared to be a pistol. I didn't have a chance to speak before the pistol came down on the side of my head. Everything went black.

I don't know how long I was out. I came to with what sounded like someone beating on a drum. My head felt like it would burst. I opened my eyes and saw nothing but darkness. I had no idea of the time and where I was. I slowly sat up, making my headache worse. And then I remembered. Someone hit me with a pistol when I was walking to my car. I vaguely remember seeing the pistol. I remember trying to get out of the way, but I obviously didn't.

I fished in my pocket for my cell phone; it could provide me with a little light. Gone. No cell phone. Whoever hit me must have taken it. I checked my back pocket for my billfold. It was there. I thought about trying to stand up, but I probably couldn't. In addition to having a splitting headache, I felt dizzy. Everything was spinning. I couldn't see anything. Couldn't even see my hand to see if the wet stuff I felt on my head was blood. I assumed it was. A wave of nausea swept over me. I felt like I might pass out again. And I was so sleepy. So very sleepy. I closed my eyes.

45
Fred and Oscar

"Well, Fred. What'd you think of this year's fair?" asked Oscar. They both attended on Friday and agreed to stop for a cup of coffee and some supper at the Black Oak Café in Link Lake before returning to their respective farms.

"It was okay," said Fred, as he wrestled with a big piece of fried cod that lay across his plate and half buried in crispy French fries. "A county fair is a county fair," he mumbled, grabbing a glass of water because he found the fish hotter than he'd anticipated. "Damned fish is hot. Good though."

"So, you've now become a philosopher," said Oscar.

"Whatta you mean by that?"

"Well, you said a county fair is a county fair. That's a kind of philosophical statement."

"A what?"

"A philosophical statement."

"Oscar, where in the hell do you get all them fifty-cent words? Do you know how to spell whatever word you just tossed at me?"

"Course I know how to spell it. What do you think I am? Dumb?" Oscar said.

"Oscar, you asked me what I thought about the fair. You don't have to get all worked up because I said it was okay. I suppose I should have said it was better than okay. Because it was."

"Well, why didn't you say that in the first place?"

"I was concentrating on eating my fish. Oscar, I think your meatloaf and mashed potatoes are gettin' cold." Fred stabbed another hunk of fried cod.

The old friends concentrated on their food for the next minute or so. Oscar broke the silence. "Fred, what is your favorite animal at the fair? Of all the animals there, from Holstein calves to rabbits, cute little lambs to hogs."

"Why you asking that? What's that got to do with the price of tea in Brazil?"

"It's price of tea in China, Fred. Price of tea in China," said Oscar.

"Why we talkin' about China? You don't know nothin' about China."

"We're not talking about China. All I asked is what animal you liked at the fair, and I gave you some examples," said Oscar.

"Well, let's see." Fred put down his fork and began mumbling something as his right hand touched each finger on his left in order. "I'd have to say the goats. I really liked them goats."

"Fred, you never had a goat on your farm; neither did I."

"Wish I had. Them goats are smart. Smarter than a damn old milk cow or a sow pig. Goats are smart as hell. Cute, too. Nothin' cuter than one of them little kids—that's what little goats are called, you know."

"I know that, Fred. Something else I know about goats?" Oscar said.

"And that would be?"

"You ever hear someone say that guy is an old goat? You ever hear that?"

"Yup, that's one of the reasons I like goats. Just the other day, I overheard a young woman talking to another young woman about an elderly gentleman she just met. She used those very words: 'elderly gentleman.' She smiled and then said the fellow was an old goat. Sounded like heartfelt words of praise to me. One of the reasons I like goats, and I must say I would look forward to being called one. High praise to be called an old goat."

"Fred, Fred, Fred, you got it backwards," said Oscar.

"Got what backwards?"

"The meaning of what the young woman said when she called the elderly gentleman an old goat," said Oscar. "Do you know what being called an old goat really means?"

"I suspect you are about to tell me," said Fred, putting the last piece of cod in his mouth.

"When someone calls you an old goat, especially a young person, it means you've done something that person thinks is stupid or just plain wrong."

"You sure about that? I've heard young people around here use those words pretty often."

"I'm sure," said Oscar. "Saying an older person is an old goat is not a form a flattery."

"There you go again, Oscar. Using some of them high falutin' words. Nobody around here talks about 'form of flattery.'"

"So, anything else about the county fair, Fred?" Oscar asked, smiling.

"I liked those little lambs, too. Cute as hell." Fred smiled from ear to ear when he said it.

46
Injury

I awakened to someone shaking my shoulder. I opened my eyes and saw Steuart, the groundskeeper for the fairgrounds.

"Scott, what are you doing here?" he asked. I now saw that I was in the storage building. With the door open I could see the riding lawnmower and an assortment of shovels, rakes, and other tools hanging on the wall.

I managed to stand by leaning on the riding lawnmower.

"What happened to you?" Steuart asked.

"Somebody hit me," I said as I felt the cut on my head. It had stopped bleeding. "Whoever it was must have dragged me in here."

The next thing I heard was Steuart on his cell phone. He must have dialed 911.

"Got an emergency at the fairgrounds, at the storage shed on the far south end. Somebody hit Scott Olson and dragged him in here."

Steuart helped me outside into the bright sun. I saw that everything was wet and glistening. I remembered coming to during the night and hearing the rain pounding on the shed's metal roof. Steuart sat me down at a picnic table. Then I heard the sound of a siren, and before I could say, "My head hurts," they had me in the ambulance and on my way to Ames County General Hospital, only a few minutes away from the fairgrounds.

I was inspected from head to toe. No broken bones. The doctor determined no concussion. I had a black eye and received four stitches in the side of my head and a prescription for some pain medicine. The doctor advised me to go home and rest.

As I was putting myself back together, Chief Wilkins rushed into the emergency room. "What in God's creation happened to you?" he asked as he saw the black eye and the bandage on my head.

"Had an unexpected surprise last night," I said, rubbing my head. The pain had subsided somewhat.

"Looks like more than a surprise. Tell me about it."

I proceeded to tell the chief about how I was walking back to my car after the fairground closed down and how someone snuck up behind me and hit me in the head with a pistol. I told him I couldn't see who it was. It was a dark, cloudy night. I explained how I tried to duck when I saw the pistol but that I obviously hadn't ducked enough.

"Geez," the chief said. "Where'd you spend the night?"

"In the storage shed."

"How'd you get in there?"

"Well, best I could figure out, after the guy—I think it was a guy—hit me, he dragged me into the shed. Steuart, the groundskeeper, must have forgotten to lock the building yesterday. I was out. Woke up when I heard it raining. Then fell back to sleep until Steuart found me."

"Scott, somebody really has it in for you. Threatening letters, somebody wanting to shoot you, and now this. I thought we'd solved the problem when we put Mike Braun in jail. Apparently not," the chief said.

Later that day, I sat in our little office at the fairgrounds. We closed the courthouse office during the duration of the fair, moving Gladys and her phone and computer into the large area. It was also a place where Sarah and I could work when we were not talking to people in the Extension booth.

Sarah was furious that I refused to take the day off and rest. She made sure I had something to eat and that I spent no time in the Extension booth but remained in the little office, away from the public. I was dozing when I heard the phone ring.

"Yes," I heard Gladys say. "Scott is here." She handed the phone to me.

"This is Bill Workman."

"What can I do for you?" I said, trying to use my professional voice but having difficulty and realizing I probably should have spent the day at home resting.

"I know you're at the fair and probably busy as all get out, but could I stop by and see you?"

"Sure, Bill. I'll be in that little office we have at the fairgrounds."

"I know where it is. I'll be there in a half hour or so."

Sarah had brought me a sandwich for lunch. It seemed every time I chewed, my head hurt. Twenty minutes later, Bill arrived.

"What in the world happened to you?" he said when he saw my black eye and the big bandage on my head.

I explained to him what happened at the fair the previous evening. I did not tell Chief Wilkins and would not tell Bill that his son, Paul, had yelled at Sarah for the work she was doing with the women in Ames County. I did not tell the chief or Bill that I had challenged him on it and that he proceeded to yell at me. And today, as I thought about it, I was quite certain it was Paul who had struck me with his pistol. I remember how angry Paul was when he left our booth last evening. I also remember someone saying that most Eagle Party members carried guns.

Bill listened carefully to my story, shaking his head the entire time. "I thought your problem was solved when the sheriff arrested Mike Braun. But apparently not," Bill said.

"I thought so, too," I said, now wondering what Bill had on his mind. I imagined he had gotten a similar email from Madison informing him, as chair of the county board's Extension committee, that each county had to cut one agent from its staff and that he wanted to talk about it.

"I've got bad news to share," Bill began. Now I was certain he was referring to the message he had received from Extension headquarters and probably wondered if Sarah or I had heard about it.

"Yes," I said, preparing for what I knew was to come. Bill, through thick and thin, year after year, had always gone to bat for the Ames County Extension Office, and for me as well as for Sarah.

"Paul has left," he said, his voice breaking.

"Left?" is all I could think to say.

"He left me a note saying he had taken a job with the Eagle Party in Indiana."

"Really. Why?"

"I don't know. We've never talked much. He and I didn't see eye to eye on many things, especially his involvement with the Eagle Party. His wife left him a couple weeks ago and told him she wanted a divorce. I'm not surprised; they didn't get along very well. She wanted a job off the farm, and he wanted none of it."

"So, what are you gonna do?" I asked, knowing that he had more work on his farm than he and his wife could handle alone.

"That's why I'm here, Scott. Do you know where I can find some help? I know good help is hard to find these days."

I thought for a bit and remembered a family that had recently arrived in the county and had stopped by the office looking for farm work. "The Pedro Gonzales family recently moved to Ames County. They have relatives here who were once migrants. Why don't you get in touch with them?"

"Are they legal? Their name sounds Mexican."

"I don't know," I said. "But they said they've had experience milking cows."

"Paul was dead set against hiring any illegal aliens, as he called them," Bill said.

He pondered my idea a bit. "You got an address or a phone number so I can get in touch with the Gonzales family?"

"Gladys has their contact information on her computer."

"Scott, thank you so much. And you take care of yourself. You tell Chief Wilkins about what happened?"

"I did," I said. Bill turned and left. There was no mention of the Extension Administration's decision to cut office staff. I wondered if he had received the message.

I left the office where Bill was talking to Gladys and returned to the Extension booth where Sarah was busy talking with people.

"What are you doing here?" she asked when she saw me. In a near whisper, she said, "You look like hell."

I whispered back, "I feel like hell."

"Then why don't you go home? You're gonna scare more people with how you look than help them."

"I'm leaving." I tried to work up a smile, but my face hurt when I did it.

"I'll bring you some supper," she said.

47
Flood

I woke up several times during the night. One time I was dreaming that Mike Braun had shot and killed Jesse Johnson, and just as he was pulling the trigger to kill me, I woke up. I was in a cold sweat and shaking. I heard heavy ground-soaking rain pounding against my bedroom window. Then I thought about this being the last day of the fair and how attendance would plummet, and the various grandstand activities would likely be canceled. Surely the vintage car race couldn't be held. Some of those old cars had difficulty traveling on dry, paved roads. A muddy race track would be more than most of them could handle.

With the rain continuing, along with the occasional flash of lightning and loud booming thunder, I finally succeeded in going back to sleep. My alarm went off at six-thirty, and I crawled out of bed and walked to my bedroom window. My headache had mostly gone, but the cut on my head still hurt, though not nearly as much as yesterday.

Following Sarah's advice, I stayed home today, watching the rain fall and thinking about why I should be at the fairgrounds. I imagined the worst. Tents, carnival rides, and outdoor displays depend on warm, sunny weather, not a continuing downpour.

Sarah stopped by in the evening with supper and shared the day's awful news. Several of the concession tents blew down. The Ferris wheel had nearly tipped over when a gust of wind caught it. All the grandstand activities were canceled, and part of the grandstand roof was destroyed. The 4-H members loaded their calves, chickens, geese, rabbits, goats—everything in the driving rain. Sarah reported that the north end of the fairgrounds, where the implement dealers had their display, was a pond with two feet of water in some places. Everybody was soaked to the skin as they worked in the driving rain.

"There were too many angry, wet people," Sarah said. "Some of them, bless their cold hearts, firmly believing that I or, maybe worse, you, had something to do with the weather."

"Some folks always have to blame someone when things go wrong," I said. "But I must say, I don't remember ever having this much rain on a fair day. I heard the weatherman on the radio say it rained six inches today. I don't remember hearing that it ever rained six inches in one day in Ames County. Ever. For the climate change deniers, today should be a wake-up call. From my take on climate change, we can look forward to more weather events like this."

"Wonder how the farmers are faring?" Sarah asked. She had set two places at the little table I had in my kitchen. She had pizza in the oven. After not having much to eat all day, it smelled divine. At least my appetite was coming back after my collision with the barrel of a pistol.

With the pizza finished, we abstained from wine because Sarah said wine and medication don't mix. Then she quietly asked, "Should we talk about the emails that we got about staff cuts?"

"Let's wait until we hear from the county administrator. I'm sure she got an email similar to the one we each got," I said.

"Okay, but we've got a lot to talk about if they cut our staff in half. Geez, neither of us has time now to do what needs to be done. How in the world can one person do it?"

After Sarah left for her cabin, with my headache almost gone, I began thinking about what would happen: Sarah or I would have to resign. Which one? We each have larger workloads than we can handle.

Feeling considerably better, I arrived at my courthouse office a bit after eight on Monday. It had rained all day Sunday and all night, and a steady rain was still falling when I parked my pickup in my assigned spot. I could imagine that phone calls and emails were already coming in from farmers and homeowners wondering what to do about flooding. Flooding was new to Ames County, consisting of mostly sandy soils that could absorb lots of rain.

"Good morning," said Gladys. "You are looking better. Black eye not so black. How you feeling?"

"Better."

I walked into my office, turned on my computer, and checked my emails. As I suspected, the majority of them were from farmers with flooded crops. I really didn't know how to answer many of them. Flooded crops were a new challenge for me. "If my carrot field is half underwater, how long before the carrots will spoil." "My green beans were ready for harvesting, and now my bean field is mostly underwater. What do I do?"

"The hail in Sunday's storm destroyed fifty acres of my sweet corn almost ready for harvesting. What do I do?"

The list of questions was never-ending. I got on the phone with the Extension vegetable specialist at Badger State University. I told her what had happened and what was continuing to happen in Ames County, as the rains had not let up, and it was now nearly noon on Monday.

"I'd like to send you the list of questions I got this morning, most of them emails, but also several phone calls. Our farmers are really upset. I'd like to prepare a news release to send to the radio station and the TV station in Green Bay. And I'd like to send it directly to the people who called in."

"I'll get right on it," the specialist said. "I'll try and have something for you by four this afternoon."

"Much appreciated," I said. Then it occurred to me. What if something like this happens when there is but one person in the office, and some calamity like this occurs? Will one already overworked agent be able to respond in a timely manner? A disaster demands an immediate response. People have come to expect that from our office.

"Bill Workman just called," Gladys said when I stopped by her desk. I told her how I had planned to handle the questions that had come in this morning, and I expected would continue to come in, especially if the rain didn't let up.

"What did Bill want?"

"He's coming in to see you and Sarah at one-thirty. I noticed you have nothing on your calendar. I've already checked with Sarah, and she's available."

"Thank you," I said. I knew what Bill wanted to talk about.

48

Tornado

Sarah and I sat in the Extension conference room, both knowing that this would likely be one of the most difficult meetings we'd ever attended.

"Geez, the rain is still coming down. Never saw anything like it in all my years of farming," Bill said. I overheard him as he talked to Gladys while hanging up his raincoat and hat.

"Good morning, Bill," I said when he came into the conference room. I stood up and shook his hand.

"Hello, Bill," Sarah said as she also stood and shook his hand.

"A little wet out your way?" I asked.

"Half my farm is underwater. When's this rain gonna stop?"

"Wish I knew," I said. "I don't think the weather people even know. I've spent all morning dealing with flood questions."

"Not surprised," Bill said. "By the way, you're looking a lot better than when I saw you last. They catch the guy who clobbered you?"

"Not yet." While recovering at home after being hit, I had decided not to tell Bill that I thought his son, Paul, may have done it and that Paul had been shouting at Sarah, and I'd called him out on it only a few minutes before I got hit. I decided not to tell Chief Wilkins my suspicions either. After all, Paul was now living in Indiana, and folks down there would have to deal with him.

"I also want you to know, Scott, that I got in touch with Pedro Gonzales as you suggested. I hired both Pedro and his wife, Isabella, to help with our milking. And I must say they are good at it. Thank you for the recommendation."

I wanted to ask if they were illegals, but I didn't.

"Oh, if you are wondering, they are both U.S. citizens, born in Brownsville, Texas. The family had been migrants for three generations, coming up here in the late 1940s to pick cucumbers."

"Glad to hear it," I said, knowing the other shoe was about to drop.

"I suspect you both know why I wanted to talk with you," Bill said. I could tell from the pained expression on his face that he'd rather be forking manure from his calf pen than talking with Sarah and me this afternoon about the email that I knew he must have received. He unfolded a sheet of paper that he took from his pocket.

"I must say," he began, " I didn't expect this. I knew the governor and the legislature had to make some budget cuts, but I couldn't imagine that they'd cut the Extension Service."

He stopped and cleared his throat. "I talked with the county administrator this morning, and I also talked with each member of the county board's Extension committee. It didn't take us long, but we quickly agreed. I called Madison to make sure that what they have suggested was the bottom line and had to happen," Bill said.

I felt myself starting to perspire and looked over at Sarah, who looked like she would be sick. I wished Bill would get on with it. Tell us which one of us is fired. Part of me was more than a little upset. With one phone call, how could they decide which of us was more needed and the other should go?

"Here's what we've decided—" he said, taking a deep breath.

Just then, the building's fire alarm went off with an ear-splitting wail. At the same time, Gladys burst into the room, screaming, "Tornado warning! Tornado warning!" Rushing out of the conference room, I could now hear the tornado siren. Bill, Sarah, and I hurried out to the hall. Courthouse employees were hurrying toward the staircases on either side of the building that led to the basement, where a utility room had been designated as a tornado shelter some years ago.

People in the neighborhood were rushing toward the courthouse as well. Everyone was carrying something. One mother carried a crying baby, an older man had what looked like a photo album, and another woman carried a rolling pin for some reason. Everyone crowded into the too-small utility room with thick concrete walls and the brick courthouse above it.

"Cell tower must be down," one fellow said as he stared at his inoperative cell phone. An older man had a battery-operated radio. In a loud voice he said, "Just heard on the Link Lake radio station that a tornado is on the ground and about five minutes outside of Willow River. It appears that Willow River will take a direct hit. Reports of severe damage to farm buildings located west of Willow River. No reports of any deaths or injuries at this time."

What next? I thought. Severe flooding and now a tornado. The room was becoming stifling hot. The two bare bulbs blinked on and off several times, then went out. The room had no windows and was immediately as dark as the darkest night. I heard someone crying. I reached out to see if Sarah was standing next to me. I touched her hand, and she grabbed hold of it.

"I'm here," she whispered.

Someone else nearby was crying. "We'll be okay," a man said.

"But what about the kids?" a woman asked.

"The kids were in the park today," another woman sobbed.

"They must have a tornado shelter at the park," the man said.

"I don't think so," she said, and her sobs became louder.

It seemed like an eternity before I heard someone opening the door to the utility room. One of Willow River's young police officers entered with a flashlight.

"It's okay to come out now. Tornado has moved east." He spoke with confidence, but I could detect more than a little concern in his voice. He had obviously seen some of the destruction the tornado left behind.

We all filed out of the room and up the stairs. Except for the power being out, everything looked like we left it. I looked out the window and saw a big oak tree had fallen across the lawn. It had hit the Civil War veteran statue that had stood on the lawn for as long as anyone could remember. It was broken into several pieces. I saw the statue's head lying off to the side, several feet away from the rest of the statue. I noticed that Bill had immediately headed for his car, no doubt worried about what damage he could expect at his farm.

The phone on Gladys's desk immediately began ringing. She started taking calls and writing down phone numbers.

49
Storm Damage

I left the office and headed for my pickup, which had been spared. Not so for several of the vehicles in the courthouse parking lot that had broken windows, one with a fallen tree across its top. I drove west out of Willow River, where the radio said the damage was greatest. Driving through Willow River, I noticed several damaged houses, one with its roof mostly torn off and another completely gone.

As I drove into the country, I saw barns down and several farm homes with trees smashed into their roofs and mile upon mile of flooded fields. As I drove into the irrigated vegetable region, I spotted an irrigation sweep with water nearly to the top of its wheels. The entire field was underwater. I couldn't even see what crop it was, but whatever it was, it was ruined. No farm crop can survive after several days underwater.

I drove by what must have been a sweet corn field, about two acres. Hail had shredded the leaves that hung lifeless against the slender stalks, some still standing in water that covered the field. Flooding and hail damage—a double whammy.

It was an eerie trip. No one was on the roads, some of which were nearly impassible with trees fallen partway across them. I stopped at Jesse Johnson's farm. He, his wife, and daughter, Aimee, were outside. I saw Aimee bending over a fallen animal. I heard her sobbing.

"Storm killed my Prince. Storm killed my horse—just got first prize for him at the fair. And now he's gone. Prince is dead. It's just not right. Not right. Prince was my friend." Aimee's whole body was shaking with grief. Her mother was trying to comfort her.

Jesse and I stood outside what had been their metal machine shed. It was a twisted mass of metal. I glanced at their farmhouse. It appeared to have been spared.

"What are you doing driving around this morning, Scott? I heard on the radio most roads were blocked."

"Doing some checking up, Jesse. Tornado hit you hard, I see." I couldn't take my eyes off a grieving Aimee stroking Prince's brown head.

"We're lucky, Scott. We're still alive. That was a killer storm. We spent the night in a storm shelter in our basement. Fortunately, my dad put it there some years ago."

"Glad to see you folks are okay, but so sorry to see what happened to Aimee's horse." That was all I could think to say. "Any idea about your crops?" I finally asked.

"Ruined. Ruined before the tornado. Fields are flooded. Potatoes are ruined. Probably all rot. Had a good crop ready for digging in a few weeks. Ruined. Had a pretty good crop of green beans. Gone. All gone." He was shaking his head in disbelief, as I figured he was just beginning to realize the depth of the storm's destruction.

"I've got to move along," I said. "I'm glad that you and your family are safe."

"Thanks for stopping, Scott. Much appreciated," Jesse said with tears in his eyes.

I'd seen enough. I drove back to Willow River and stopped at the cell phone store—downtown Willow River had been spared from the tornado, and the electricity was back on. I bought a new cell phone. The guy who hit me on the head must have taken mine before he stuffed me in the storage shed at the fairgrounds. I returned to my office and prepared for a very busy day. I had no time to think about the reorganization of our office.

"How bad is it?" Sarah asked as I came through the door.

"It's bad. Fields flooded. Buildings destroyed. Homes without roofs. Saw several homes with trees that had crashed into them. The west side of Willow River was hit pretty bad, too. Guessing a lot of folks without a dry place to sleep tonight," I said.

"Phone calls keep coming in," said Gladys. "What are we gonna do?"

"Fair's just over. Let's open up a couple buildings at the fairgrounds so people with destroyed houses will have a place to sleep. Fairground buildings were mostly spared. We can use the 4-H food building as a place to prepare meals," I said. "Gladys, would you contact the radio station in Link Lake? Let them know that people hit by the storm will have a place to eat and a place to sleep."

"Good idea, Scott. I'll see if I can round up some 4-H leaders and some Homemaker members to help. The tornado missed the east end of the county, and they haven't had as much flooding either," Sarah said.

I got on the phone with the local Red Cross Emergency Center and explained what we planned to do at the fairgrounds. They said they'd bring blankets and cots to the fairgrounds, and their volunteers would also help with food preparation.

I called members of the planning council and asked them if they would be willing to help out. Several said they would drop what they were doing and hurry to the fairgrounds. Both Emil and Bill said they had some minor wind damage at their farms, mostly tree limbs down, but nothing as serious as I reported had happened at Jesse's place. Each said, "Count on me to help out." I called Steuart at the fairgrounds to open a couple of buildings and explained what our plans were.

I drove out to the fairgrounds. The Red Cross was already there, unloading blankets and cots and setting them up in the big horticulture building with tables still filled with vegetables, flowers, and field crop exhibits from over the weekend. The sweet smell of flowers still hung in the air.

A couple of 4-H leaders had the cookstove going in the 4-H food building. I could smell fresh coffee brewing. "Hi, Scott," one of the

4-H leaders said. "Ready for your mid-morning coffee?"

"Thanks, no," I said. "Maybe later."

Later that afternoon, the first storm victims began arriving at the fairgrounds, tired and dirty, some with scratches and bruises that were immediately cared for by EMTs who agreed to stay as long as they were needed.

A yellow school bus stopped in front of the horticulture building and began unloading people whose homes had been destroyed by the storm—men, women, crying children—all stunned but happy to be alive. I'd just heard on the radio that five people had been reported dead. Three people in one family, living in a trailer court on the west side of Willow River, died in the storm when their mobile home was demolished. They had no time to escape to the trailer court's concrete laundry building designated as a tornado shelter.

Another school bus arrived. I quickly learned that it contained senior citizens from the assisted living center on the west side of town. The tornado had torn most of the roof from the building. Volunteers were helping each of them off the bus and into the horticulture building. They looked dazed. One woman was mumbling, "Why are we here? Take me home. Take me home."

On one end of the big building, I spotted Sarah and her crew of volunteers setting up tables for serving food. Almost immediately, the first tables had storm survivors sitting at them, eating food the volunteers were preparing in the 4-H food building. Sarah told me that some of them hadn't had anything to eat since yesterday.

As I walked around, helping where needed and answering questions when I could, I realized that I was seeing city and country people, small-acreage farmers and large commercial farmers all working together, helping to set up cots and serve food. I even saw several lake property owners from Winter Lake helping out. George Emerson must have passed along the word that volunteers were needed. Property owners worked with the very farmers they believed they hated because of what their irrigation practices were doing to their lake levels. I thought, *As bad as this storm has been, some good may be coming from it.*

50
Mystery Solved

The week flew by. I spent as much time as possible at the fairgrounds and was pleased that by week's end, everyone who we had sheltered and fed had found a place to stay—most of them in their own homes that were repaired enough to move back in them.

I also tried to answer unending questions about what to do with flooded fields and hail-destroyed crops. Thankfully, the following week's weather was clear, sunny, and in the eighties, with a slight southerly breeze. Good drying weather. I'd nearly forgotten the meeting Sarah and I had with Bill Workman when the tornado alert sounded. It all came back quickly when Gladys said, "Bill Workman is on the phone."

"Hello, Bill," I answered.

"We need to follow up on that meeting that you, Sarah, and I had last week. Would you and Sarah have time this afternoon, say around three?"

I said I would check with Sarah and ask Gladys to call back. I wasn't looking forward to the meeting. I remember so well the email both Sarah and I had gotten, and I assume a similar one arrived at Bill's computer. Either Sarah or I would have to go. It just wasn't fair. I was thinking of Brown County, where they had six agents. Dropping one would be one-sixth of their staff. Laying off one of our staff of two meant dropping half of our staff.

Sarah was available to meet, and promptly at three o'clock, Bill arrived. He carried some papers that he placed in front of him on the conference table.

"First," he began, "thank you for all that you did in helping the citizens of Ames County deal with some of the worst storm damage I can remember. I don't think we ever had a week of torrential rain followed by a tornado. What you both did, especially at the fairgrounds, was outstanding."

We both said thank you, anxious to get the bad news out on the table so we could discuss how we would deal with it.

"You both got an email similar to the one that I have, instructing us to cut our Extension Office by one person."

"Yes, we did," I said, hoping that Bill would quit beating around the bush and let us get his and the Extension committee's reaction to the email.

"Our committee met for three hours on this question, and I have been instructed to share our decision with you."

So far, he was giving no hint of what that decision was and whether they had decided which one of us should go.

"We have decided ..." he hesitated for a moment. "We have decided to not cut a position from our staff."

"But don't you have to?" I blurted, remembering that the email left no room for doubt of the intent.

"As it turns out, if Ames County is willing to pay the salary and benefits for one of its Extension agents, we have the right to do that," Bill said. "So, you both have jobs and can quit worrying."

"Thank you," Sarah said. I could see tears in her eyes.

"Thank you for your support." I shook Bill's hand. "Thank you so much."

Bill got up to leave, and once more, each of us shook his hand. Sarah and I shared the good news that both of us would continue as Extension agents in Ames County and would not be following the state budget cuts that demanded each county reduce its agent staff by one person.

"Well, I must be getting on home. Lots of storm cleanup to do. Glad I could bring you good news," Bill said as he left the conference room.

Returning to my office, I no more than turned to my computer when the phone rang.

"It's Ann Arnold from the police department," Gladys said.

"Hello, Ann. What can I do for you?"

"Got a few minutes for me to stop by your office and talk?"

"Sure," I said.

Fifteen minutes later, Officer Arnold sat across from me at my desk.

"What's up?" I asked.

"I have good news. I heard from the crime lab in Madison this morning, and we know who threw the rock through the window."

With all that had been going on—the flood, the tornado, and the threat of the office losing half its staff—I'd almost forgotten about the rock incident and the two letters.

"It's pretty interesting what the lab folks found. They discovered that the paper used for both letters was a special paper made only by one paper mill in Neenah. The paper had a watermark, which led them to the paper mill. Investigators traveled to Neenah and, from the paper mill officials, learned the names of the distributors that sold this special paper."

I listened patiently to the details of the investigation, but I wanted to know the person's name. I was guessing it was probably Mike Braun. He was my prime candidate.

"Well," Officer Arnold continued. "The investigators learned that only three office supply stores in Wisconsin carried this special paper and that the customers for the paper were law offices and financial institutions. They got the names of customers who had purchased this special paper. And guess what?"

"What?" I said, hoping she'd tell me the name of the culprit who had threatened me.

"The Ames County Bank was one of the customers."

"Really," was all I could think to say. Now I was wondering if the crime lab had screwed up. How could Mike Braun have gotten this special paper from the bank?

"Now the crime lab turned to the fingerprints. They found some good, usable prints on the second message to you. As part of the bank's background check for bonding its employees, they fingerprint them. And they found a match."

"Who?" I blurted out.

"The person who threw the rock through the community building window with the letter to you and the follow-up letter were written by none other than Jeff Miles, the loan officer at the bank."

"Are you sure?"

"The evidence doesn't lie."

"But why? Why would Jeff Miles do such a thing?" I asked, still trying to wrap my mind around the fact that he was the one who had done it.

"I guess you'll have to ask him why he did. That we don't know."

"So, what's next?" I asked.

"Well, I stopped here to see if you wanted to press charges concerning the threatening letters. Our judgment was by themselves the letters didn't rise to criminal activity. But you could press charges of harassment if you chose to do so."

"No, no. I don't want to press charges. I still can't believe that Jeff did it. I've been working with him all summer. I thought we got along just fine."

"Well, okay," said Officer Arnold. "But I'm going to stop at the bank when I leave here and arrest Miles for destruction of public property. It's a misdemeanor and will probably only result in a fine."

"Thank you for letting me know," I said. "But I still can't believe he did it." Officer Arnold got up and left the office.

I sat back in my chair, thinking, *How could this be? Why would Jeff Miles send me those nasty letters?* I walked out to where Gladys sat.

"What did the police officer want?"

"Let's go into Sarah's office. I want you both to hear this." I wondered how Sarah would react to the news. After all, she and Jeff Miles had dated when they were both in college.

Epilogue

Once the three of us were seated in Sarah's office, I began with the old cliché, "I have good news and bad news."

"The good news is Officer Arnold just told me who threw the rock through the community building with the nasty note attached and who left a second note at our office. I began by telling them the process the crime lab in Madison had used in identifying the culprit, as Officer Arnold had explained to me. I quickly noticed that they were much more interested in who did it rather than how the crime lab figured out who did it.

"This brings me to the bad news. The person who did it is Jeff Miles."

"Can't be," blurted Gladys.

"Are you sure?" Sarah asked.

I explained that Officer Arnold was '100 percent sure they had identified the right person, and she was on her way to the bank right now to arrest him.

"Oh, no," said Gladys, who began to cry. I had not expected this reaction from her.

"Scott, Sarah," Gladys began. Sarah had handed her a tissue to wipe her eyes.

"Jeff Miles is my nephew," she said. "My sister's son. This is awful, just awful. You both deserve to know what happened. But I still can't believe he wrote those letters. It's just not like him. I still can't believe it."

Sarah and I were both stunned by what we were hearing.

"Jeff had called me before he took the job at the bank and said he knew Sarah worked in the Extension Office, and he still loved her, and he wanted to resume their relationship," Gladys said. "Don't take this wrong, but I knew something was going on between the two of you soon after Sarah arrived. I didn't tell anybody, and I know you were trying to be discrete, but you just can't hide some things."

I looked at Sarah. She smiled, but neither of us said anything.

"Anyway," Gladys continued, "I told Jeff that the two of you appeared to have more than just a friendly professional relationship in the office. I had no idea he would write those nasty letters to you, Scott. No idea."

"Love takes some unusual turns," I said. Why I said that, I will never know. I was clearly the last person to know about the various turns love takes. Sarah rolled her eyes when I said it, confirming what I was already thinking.

"Believe me, I knew nothing about the letters," Gladys said. Then she began crying again. "Do you want me to resign?"

"Gladys, we do not want you to resign. This office would collapse without you. I believe you," I said.

"I tried to let Jeff know that he should move on. Find someone else—apparently he has. Someone said they'd seen him and Jill Varsac together several times," said Gladys.

"Well, I told Officer Arnold that I would not press charges concerning the letters, but she said she had to arrest him for throwing a rock through the window of a public building, which was a misdemeanor and would result in a fine."

Three days later, a very sorry-looking Jeff Miles appeared in my office. I heard him say hello to Gladys before entering, but no more.

"Jeff," I said. "How are you doing?"

"Not so well." This was not the confident Jeff Miles I had worked with all summer and who had made several important contributions to our planning council.

"As you now know, I was the guy who wrote those nasty letters to you, Scott. I am truly sorry. It was the dumbest thing I ever did. By far." He looked like he was going to cry.

"When the bank found out, they immediately fired me. Can't blame them. I've paid my fine for the broken window. I don't know what I was thinking." He paused for a minute and took a deep breath. "Scott, you are a good man. You and Sarah make a great team. I am so, so sorry for all of this."

"Thank you, Jeff," I said. "What are your plans?"

"I don't know what to do. I can't stay in Willow River. I will have zero credibility once the paper comes out with all this. I haven't told Jill about all of this. I'm thinking of moving to Alaska, starting over again."

"Good luck to you, and thanks for stopping by. I'll miss your good work on the council."

He got up and walked to the door, his head down and shoulders slumped. I heard him say goodbye to Gladys as he left the office.

How the year has flown by. First, I should report that Sarah and I were married in October. We chose to marry at the park in Willow River. It was a beautiful fall day. The maples and aspen were in peak color, and I have never seen a more beautiful Sarah. We put a notice in the paper that anyone who wanted to attend the event was welcome. We were both surprised by how many people turned out. I closed down my apartment and moved into Sarah's cabin at the lake.

On this cool April day, with rain splashing against the community center's windows, the Ames County Agricultural Council is holding its first annual meeting. The group's core members were a part of the Ames County Agricultural Planning Council. They have dropped "planning" from their title, have drawn up a constitution, elected officers, and have invited anyone "with any interest" in agriculture to join.

Sarah and I are sitting in the back of the room. I counted some 150 people in attendance. No one wore a special shirt or cap or carried a placard. President Jodi Henderson is at the podium welcoming everyone and then asking for committee reports from the various work groups the council has organized.

I sat listening and thinking. Ames County has a long way to go in ironing out the differences between the lake owners and the large commercial farmers who irrigate with deep-well pumps. With all the rain and flooding, Winter Lake has come back a bit this past year—so the complaints from the lake owners are a bit less than they were a year ago. I noticed that several lake property owners were in the audience, paying members of the council.

I thought back to a year ago, when the rock came crashing through the window, and the meeting I'd organized quickly fell apart. How far we'd come in just one year. But it was not without its problems. I thought back to Jeff Miles and how a couple of foolish mistakes ruined a promising career.

But even with all the problems with the weather, the budget, protests, and angry people, the people of Ames County are good people, willing to help each other when there is trouble.

Above all, as I think back over the year, the high point was my marriage to Sarah. Sarah said it was for her, too.

Acknowledgments

Writing a novel requires the help of many. First, I want to thank my late wife Ruth, who passed away during the time that I was working on this book. She, herself an extension agent at one time, offered many suggestions on what to include. We first met when I was an extension agent in Green Lake County, and she was an extension agent in Waushara County, a neighboring county to the north. My daughter Susan, an author of several books, and an excellent editor, helped me more than she will ever know as I continued writing after Ruth's passing. Natasha Kussulke, my daughter-in-law, a trained journalist, provided many useful tips including the title for the book. Steve, her husband and my son offered many big picture ideas for the story. From his office in Colorado, my other son, Jeff, patiently listened when I shared several of my concerns about the book with him. And lastly, I can't say enough of how I appreciate the hard work of Kristin Mitchell and her staff at Little Creek Press for agreeing to publish this work, and provide several ideas for making my rough draft manuscript better. Thank you.

About the Author

Jerry Apps was born and raised on a farm in central Wisconsin. Upon graduation from the University of Wisconsin-Madison, and spending time in the U.S. Army, Apps worked as a county extension agent in Green Lake and Brown County Wisconsin. He then worked as a staff development specialist for the University of Wisconsin-Extension. He is Professor Emeritus of the University Wisconsin-Madison and the author of several fiction and non-fiction books about agriculture and rural life in the Upper Midwest.

Book Club Questions

1. Scott Olson is the County Agricultural Agent for Ames County. How did he attempt to bring people together as part of his job? Which ways seemed to be successful?

2. Jodi is a small acreage farmer in the county. How does this character become essential to the plot as the story progresses?

3. To what extent do Fred and Oscar's coffee shop meetings help move the plot forward?

4. How did the author portray the importance of having an extension office in a rural community?

5. Which characters surprised you the most? Were there any you could relate to?

6. What were the main themes or messages of the book? Was there anything that surprised you?

7. What ideas will you continue to think about?

Printed in the United States
by Baker & Taylor Publisher Services